ACCIDENTAL AF

THE ACCIDENTALS

BOOK 13

DAKOTA CASSIDY

D1528347

ABOUT THIS BOOK

A stranded human and his lifelong skepticism walk into a paranormal bar...

Sounds like the start of a bad gag, but the joke's on Kash Samuels when he stumbles into a bar called NOPE, looking for warmth and a working phone, only to get caught in the middle of a bar fight. Next thing you know, he's got weird...appendages...popping up all over the place...a fin here, a lock of pink hair there, a mangy tail somewhere else...

Maybe he actually fell asleep in his car and the exhaust fumes made him loco. It's the only way to explain the insanity that ensues when he finds himself surrounded by a group of stunning ladies claiming to be paranormal beings, along with their entourage of demon, zombie, and troll butler/chef. And let's not even discuss the line around the block of other supernatural species, each hoping to claim Kash as their own...

Oh, and one totally crush-worthy human scientist. A woman Kash is falling for more every day. Too bad she's keeping him at arm's length—and in the dark about her own health, even as she works day and night to help Kash control his wonky body.

Yep, life sure has taken a turn. For Kash, who's always wanted a family after growing up in the system, just him and his brother against the world, this kind and crazy group may not be the family he envisioned...but they're the family you need when you're Accidental AF!

COPYRIGHT

DEDICATION

Darling readers,

Welcome to Accidental number 48901673... LOL! Seriously, welcome back, friends! For the first time in the history of the Accidentals, we have a man on the cover. It was time to give this whacky world I've created a shakeup.

A couple of things: First, thank you for coming back. I don't know what brings you back, but it means the world to me that you return time and again. Second, the paranormal "disease" in this edition is complete fiction, concocted solely for the purpose of this story, during a late-night phone conversation with my BFF Renee George (read her books!), with whom I plot all my books.

That said, you'll see some old friends from prior books and meet some new ones. I hope you have as much fun reading this as I did writing it!

Love,
Dakota XXOO

CHAPTER

ONE

K ash Samuels kicked rocks along the dark, dusty road, cursing his brother Garrick for not replacing the spare tire the last time he'd borrowed his car.

It was a sweet ride, for sure, and he'd reluctantly allowed Garrick to borrow it to impress a woman with the promise he'd return it without a spark plug out of place.

And he had. Mostly. He should have known better than to expect Garrick not to cut corners or forget something as important as replacing a spare tire kit. He should have given his car a thorough once over before taking it on a road trip.

That, coupled with the fact that his cell refused to cooperate and give him even half a bar, and only when he held it facing north with his right arm in the air, left him madder than a one-armed boxer.

He didn't even really know where he was. He'd definitely made a wrong turn somewhere along the way. His navigation had obviously failed, but he'd been lost in thought about the possibility of an overseas business venture as his car ate up the miles, and he'd soon lost track of where he was before he'd realized he'd gone the wrong way.

There was hope, though. A light not too far down the road shined with a faded yellow flicker.

With not a road sign in sight, on foot, he headed toward the light like a moth to a flame. Tucking his chin into his jacket, Kash braced himself against the bitter cold and plodded forward, his boots crunching against the frozen November ground.

As he approached what looked like the shittiest shack he'd ever seen, the barn wood rotted in places and the solitary window boarded up, he took note of the neon sign.

It read simply, "NOPE," all in capital letters.

Was that the name of the bar? Was it even a bar? From the short distance, it sure sounded like a bar. He definitely heard music and some banging around, maybe a bit of raucous laughter.

But what a weird name for a bar...

Yet the name wasn't going to stop him. He needed something searing and warm in his gut and a phone. A whiskey neat sounded about right. He'd pay double for one if it meant he could warm the hell up.

Kash stopped in the dirt parking lot, clenching his

icy fingers into a fist as he looked around to survey his surroundings. There weren't very many cars for so much damn noise. As he got closer, he distinctly heard Vivaldi's *The Four Seasons* playing.

A place called NOPE couldn't be all that bad if it had Vivaldi on the jukebox, right?

NOPE was shrouded in trees—big pines, winter-bare maples and oaks—leading him to think maybe it was an exclusive club. Maybe inside it was posh and the name and appearance were to discourage nonmembers from entering?

But an exclusive club way out here? In the middle of Nowheresville, NY? Though, Kash thought, that sort of made sense. A bar for illicit activity, tucked away where no one could find it.

But he didn't want to walk in on some kind of *Eyes Wide Shut* sitch. He liked some spice. However, not quite *that* much spice.

Yet, the couple of cars in the parking lot didn't suggest it was an exclusive place. The '71 Oldsmobile looked as though it'd been through the mill, and though the red Prius was nice and well-maintained, it didn't scream rich and private...

Kash planted his hands on his hips and eyed the place one more time before walking up to the rickety wooden entrance, broken and rotted in spots.

His gut said one thing, but frostbite called and said something altogether different.

So he pushed his way through the groaning door—

and instantly, everyone, young and old alike, turned around to look at him.

Fuck.

His first observation? This wasn't an *Eyes Wide Shut* crowd. No matter how much Vivaldi drifted through the air from the ancient jukebox in the corner, these men didn't come across as, for lack of a better word, sophisticated.

Not judging from all the ruggedly worn jeans, facial hair and greasy coifs.

But who the hell was he to judge? He'd learned a long time ago the theory about books and their covers.

Either way, he had two choices. One, get out. Die a hero of the elements.

Or two, walk directly up to the bar as though he wasn't worried the entire place would erupt in chaos and chew him a new asshole, slam his hand down on the surface, and demand a whiskey neat.

Inhaling, Kash decided he was used to fighting. As an ex-foster kid who'd aged out of the system, he'd been in plenty of fights—many because of, or in defense of, his brother.

Kash Samuels knew how to take care of his own.

So, while everyone stared at him, while there wasn't a sound but the Vivaldi playing, he sauntered up to the greasy bar, littered with peanut shells and broken pretzels, and grabbed a seat, sliding in next to an enormous man who was, of all things, eating a crepe with lavish pleasure.

The man looked up for a moment and sniffed the air next to Kash, his wide but pleasant face frowning. Then he shook his dark head not quite covered in a knit Giant's hat, nodded to him in acknowledgement, and went back to eating his crepe, while Kash set about getting the bartender's attention.

He raised his hand to catch the skinny guy's notice, but he appeared distracted by something that was happening at the back of the bar in a dark corner.

Kash couldn't see what was going on, but he could definitely hear a heated discussion taking place.

"Shut the fucking-fuck up, Rozwell! Don't you talk about my girl like that!"

"Aw, piss off, Gorkowski. I'm your best friend. I'm just tryin' to keep you from gettin' your ass stomped on all over again. She's an *ogre*, dude. Everybody knows fucking ogres are cheaters and liars!"

An ogre? What an interesting way to describe your best friend's girlfriend. Garrick had called Kash's last girlfriend, also a liar and a cheat, many things, but he'd never used the word ogre.

"Say it one more time, Roz," the man threatened, as now the eyes of everyone in the place turned from burning holes in Kash's back to the argument between two friends. "One more time and fuck friendship, I'll wipe your ass up one end of this bar and down the other. You got that, fucker?"

Kash didn't turn around. He knew when to mind his business, especially when it came to a woman, but he heard the growl in the guy's voice and it was a clear warning. So he kept his ear cocked and his senses on alert.

"I'm not lettin' it go, Gork," the other man insisted, his tone half-pleading, half-annoyed. "I know what the hell I saw, and I saw that beast with Langston Pickney over at Houston's. I saw her, I tell you!"

"Houston's? *The friggin' vampire bar*?" Gorkowski squawked. "The fuck you say. Ogre's and vampires never mingle, dumbass. Now I know you're lyin' about her!"

Kash continued to keep his head down, staring at the sticky bar's surface, but he had to wonder if vampires and ogres was some sort of new slang for a cheating girlfriend he'd somehow missed on his Twitter timeline.

"He ain't lyin'," yet another man defended with a booming voice. "I saw her, too, Roz."

"I said you better shut the fuck up—both of you," Gorkowski bellowed. "One more word and I'm gonna smash your heads together!"

These two knuckleheads didn't know when to shut up, did they? It was clear this man was beyond agitated, yet they continued to goad him.

And Gork wasn't lying when he'd made it clear one more word would set him off, because when one of the men said, "Roz," all bloody hell broke loose.

Kash heard a primal scream of a roar, one that sounded almost inhuman. He turned around, plan-

6

ning to get the hell out, but the whole bar became a clusterfuck of bodies swarming one another—facing off, staring each other down, almost as if there were sides to be taken.

Bodies packed together and that's when he heard the first punch thrown, sharp and clear and then...

Well, then shit happened.

Somehow, instead of inching his way out of the suddenly tight space, Kash ended up in the middle of the fray. Flashes of angry faces narrowed in on him as every man in the bar rushed at each other like some kind of greasy, hairy version of *West Side Story*.

The piercing-hot sting of something sinking into his thigh jerked him into motion. He didn't know what it was. Knife? Razor blade? He couldn't be sure, but he wasn't gonna stick around to find out. It was time to hightail it the fuck out of there.

Kash gave a shove with everything he had against the wall of men, but to no avail.

He didn't think it was possible for every soul in the bar to be stronger than him, but it was looking like this bunch didn't just sit around and eat crepes all day because they were almost immovable.

Someone slammed him up against the bar top, bending him backward until he thought his spine would snap. Groaning, he tried to push his way back up, but all the sit-ups he did in the gym were obviously for naught. The guy on top of him didn't move until he decided he wanted to move, and even then, he climbed over Kash's body and onto the bar, stepping on his jaw with a grind of his booted heel along the way.

There was another flash of something sharp and gleaming under the neon Jack Daniels sign, and his neck went rigid with a fierce pain he had to believe was more than a pulled muscle, but he didn't have time to think about it much as a ball of fire hurtled toward him at warp speed.

There but for the grace of whoever's in charge of the universe, Kash was able to slide down to the floor and duck the stream of flames, but that didn't help as much as one would think.

Because now he was on the floor being trampled.

Hands tore at his flesh as they scurried to get over him and stand upright. He heard the distinct tear of his jeans, felt the rip of his skin and the burn of flesh that followed.

At this point, his body was on fire, engulfed in some weird limbo of agony and paralysis. Kash struggled to focus as the chaos above him raged.

He heard foul words as though they were whispered directly into his ear.

Surges of electricity coursed through his bloodstream as if someone injected him with hot rushes of vinegar water.

And hair.

There was hair?

Holy cow. Yep. They were definitely tufts of hair he

saw floating in the air only to land on his face, tickling his nose and grazing his cheek.

Kash didn't simply see the hair, either—he saw every single strand, so magnified, if he had the notion, he could count them.

That was crazy, but he didn't have time to reflect on that before he felt a slap of something cold and... and *scaly* against his cheek and then the scent of fish wafted to his nostrils.

Had someone hit him with a fish? What the *fuck* was going on?

Still, he couldn't move enough to find out. His muscles tightened almost unbearably, becoming so rigid, he thought surely they would snap and spring from his body as his legs and arms twisted into shapes he didn't know were even possible.

Yet, he otherwise couldn't move, let alone get out of the way of all the bodies slamming into him.

And then like some kind of oversized angel from Heaven, a shadowy figure with two hands the width of sides of beef grabbed him, hurling his limp, unresponsive body over a cushiony shoulder and running with him toward the door as Vivaldi still streamed in Kash's ears.

Looking back now, he should have gone with his gut and froze to death.

Fuck, he *really* should have gone with his gut.

CHAPTER
TWO

The woman named Nina, so beautiful Kash almost couldn't fathom she was real, stood over him, her mouth hanging open.

Her potty mouth, that is.

He'd never heard anyone swear the way she did. Not even when he'd done a stint in the Marines. It was a cavalcade of one expletive after another while she gazed at him with menacing coal eyes the shape of almonds and a sneer on her lush lips.

But he had to admit, if there was ever anything to swear about, this'd be the thing.

A tall young man with dark hair, pale green skin and duct tape wrapped around his middle finger glanced with obvious curiosity over Nina's shoulder.

His skin was green. *Green.*

Good fuck, what was happening?

"What the actual fuck?" Nina asked in a husky

voice, tucking her almost waist-length silky dark hair behind her ears, before she looked to the enormous mountain of a man named Darnell.

Kash's official forever hero.

Darnell.

The hush of Darnell's soft voice betrayed his tall, beefy size, which is what had convinced Kash to leave the bar with him in his little red Prius. Because Darnell's voice had soothed the raging tide in his head and the hot flashes scorching throughout his limbs.

Not that he'd had much choice anyway.

He crossed his colossal arms over his even bigger chest, and tucking his thumbs under his armpits, he said, "I told y'all on the phone, Boss. This is crazy, right? Cain't say I ever saw nothin' like it."

"The craziest," cooed the pretty woman who had introduced herself as Marty, who was all sparkly jewelry and five different shades of blonde, peering at him from sapphire-blue eyes fringed in long lashes.

Nina clucked her tongue and frowned, inspecting Kash from head to toe. "Look, I'm just gonna call this shit now, m'kay? He's got more problems than three bitches like us can handle. I say we take his ass home, wherever that is, drop him off, tuck him in and make him some warm milk or what-the-fuck-ever you sensitive nutballs do to soothe a dude with this much shit going on, and go home. We don't have the skills to fix this kind of fucknuttery."

The sophisticated lady who stood so regally in a

slim gray skirt and ice-blue silk shirt gasped. Her name was Wanda, and she had a lovely, lilting tone to her voice that was as sophisticated as she looked.

Her eyes went wide, then they narrowed. "Did you really just say that to us, Nina? *Really*?"

She shook her dark head, ebony hair falling all around her shoulders and down her back. She drove her hands into her hoodie pockets and nodded. "Yeah. I fuckin' did. This is meant for bigger bitches than us."

"There *are* no bigger bitches than us. We're it, and you know it," Marty retorted, shaking her finger at Nina, making her bracelets jingle with a sound so loud, Kash had to fight not to cover his ears and curl up in a protective ball.

Jesus Christ, his senses were so acute, so sensitive, it was like he was seeing sounds and hearing colors.

While Marty continued to give Nina a piece of her mind, it was at that moment he finally lost it. Granted, you'd think he told them they were all ugly shrews and sure, it turned out to be an enormous fuck-up on his part, but it did successfully quiet everyone down.

"Could you please stop yelling, lady?" Kash virtually begged, his voice sounding raspy and desperate to his ears.

There was a silence so rich in its quiet, he thought he heard someone's hair growing.

That is, until it went left, anyway. Then it was all gasps and assholes and elbows, and the young man someone had called Carl widened his eyes in horror.

Nina grabbed him by the collar of his shirt and hauled him off Wanda's soft couch, placing him so close to her face, he saw she had no pores. Not a one.

How was that even possible to get to her age with no pores? She was easily in her late twenties. Didn't she ever have acne like the rest of the teenage population?

And by hell, she was strong. Insanely strong. She was holding him up with one hand and his feet were no longer touching the ground. *One* hand.

Kash stopped worrying about her pores and her strength when, with clear venom, she hissed, "Buddy I'm gonna..." But then she trailed off, her voice becoming vague, leaving him confused.

She'd come at him hot, but somewhere between grabbing him and preparing a verbal threat, she looked like she'd lost her steam.

In what appeared to be frustration, Nina's nostrils flared and she flashed her...

No. He couldn't think it. He wouldn't.

Think it, Kash! Go on! Do it. I know it makes it real, but by God, it is *real. It's the only way to accept what you're seeing.*

He closed his eyes and swallowed so hard, he heard his own gulp.

Fine. This beautiful monster is flashing her fangs at me.

F-A-N-G-S spells fangs.

Use it in a sentence, Kash. C'mon. You can do it.

Fine. Nina has fangs.

Well done, Kashster! Cue polite golf clap.

"Nina?" the blonde woman named Marty squeaked, the expression on her face perplexed.

"What?" Nina bellowed back with a roar fashioned to wake the dead.

"You forgot to finish your threat," she reminded her with a giggle-snort, planting her hands on her hips in some sort of silent challenge. "What comes after the immortal words, 'Buddy, I'm gonna...'? Was it kill you in your sleep? No wait, I know, I'll rip your leg off and beat your ass with it? Or my favorite, I'll use your nads to make pate served on those fancy little paper-thin crackers."

Carl snickered, but muffled the sound by placing his arm over his mouth.

Nina glared at Marty, her jaw going tight, yet still she said nothing.

Marty's eyes narrowed in succinct suspicion. "Okay, what's happening here? Is this what some would call an epiphany, Mistress of the Dark? Or are we in an alternate dimension and somebody forgot to tell me we've been wormhole jumping?"

Nina shot her a look of pure disgust, still not loosening her grip on Kash. "Fuck you, Blondie. Forgive me if I'm a little shooketh. I mean, look at this motherfucker, would you? Jesus effin' Christ, he's a damn mess. For the first time in a long time, I'm so shook, I don't even have the fucking energy to threaten someone."

She was right. He felt like a damn mess. He was shooketh, too.

Kash ran a hand over his face, which was on fire with rushes of flaming heat, trying to avoid Nina's hand on the lapel of his jacket.

"I apologize, Miss...Statleon, did you say? I didn't mean to yell. It was rude."

He didn't care if his balls had just shrunk up to tiny raisins for apologizing either. He wasn't a moron. Nina was hella scary and hella strong.

But so were Marty and Wanda. They both grabbed an arm and pulled Nina away until he fell back on the puffy couch in a pile of limbs—or whatever it was you called what he had now.

A fin, Kash. You have a fin. It's only one, and it's sticking out of the side of your leg, but it's definitely a fin. You also have a tail. A bushy, furry tail.

Wanda popped her lips and gave Nina a stern look. "Nina. Just once, could you not choose violence before we're even ten minutes into the interview? Lay off. The man's in shock."

Hashtag facts. Shock was likely understating his condition, but it was close enough and he was damn grateful for Wanda's intervention.

Nina growled, yanking a piece of his hair and holding it up under the glow of a lamp before she dropped it.

Wait. Had he seen that right? Kash looked down at the strand, now lying on his chest. That hair was pink...and long...and curly—but his hair was short, dark, and straight. Yet, he knew it was his hair because when she'd tugged the pink strand, Kash felt it.

What the absolute fuck?

And stop the presses. Why couldn't he take his eyes off the pulse beating in Marty's neck. How could he hear her blood thrum through her veins? Why did it make his mouth water and his palms sweat?

Kash could almost taste her soft flesh against his lips as his teeth sank into her creamy skin.

Leaning back into the couch, he took deep breaths, praying the crazy craving to put his mouth on her neck and bite would pass.

The craving was far worse than when he'd quit smoking ten years ago.

As if smoking and taking a bite out of someone's neck were even in the same stratosphere. *Jesus, Kash. Batten down your shit!*

Marty sat next to him on the cushy couch, making him want to jump out of his skin. She patted his hand. "You want to bite me, don't you?"

Horrified and riddled with guilt, Kash's eyes went wide as she tapped her neck. Licking his dry lips, he tried to find his words, to no avail.

She smiled at him, a smile filled with warm sympathy. "It's okay, Kash. It was an easy deduction. I'm technically the only one with a pulse and heartbeat here. Wanda doesn't count because she's only a halfsie and her organs aren't as strong as mine."

He frowned and blinked. "A *what*?"

Wanda plopped down on the other side of him and smiled, too. "How about we focus on what's happening now and have a lesson in paranormal lingo later? Instead, why don't you tell us how this... happened. I mean, in your words."

Kash opened his mouth to speak, but for the second time, words escaped him.

Wanda put her finely boned fingers under his chin and pushed, effectively closing his mouth. "It's a lot to take in, Kash. Believe me, we all understand. Just take your time."

But Kash couldn't summon words. He couldn't even summon syllables...

Carl reached a hand over and patted his arm with a thump, shooting him a sympathetic look.

Darnell sat on the thick wood coffee table in front of him and looked him in the eye. "You want me to tell 'em for ya, brother? I mean, I did see it all."

Kash shrugged. It was all he was capable of because his body was on fire and his back itched as though a thousand fire ants were crawling along his spine.

Darnell held up his hands, palms facing Kash. "You can trust us, man. Swear it."

Kash simply nodded. It was all he could manage as

he fought to control his body, tensing and flexing in almost painful contractions.

Darnell sighed and looked to the women. "So here's what happened, best I can tell. This poor guy's car broke down. He walked until he found NOPE—"

Wanda gasped, the hiss in Kash's ears shrill and cutting. "No. No-no. Oh, Heaven have mercy. Not NOPE. That filthy toxic waste of a bar? Ugh! It's a breeding ground for the paranormal scourge of the earth."

Kash vaguely remembered walking into the bar, but he couldn't seem to remember much after that. He'd have to rely on Darnell's memory to explain, but for sure, he didn't remember the scourge, paranormal or otherwise.

He just remembered a lot of burly, hairy guys and one or two women...

Darnell pulled his knit cap off and tucked it between his big knees. "Yep. And I think y'all know, it ain't a place no human should be, that's for sure. Anyhow, he went up to the bar and was gonna order a drink and it got real quiet. I thought sure as I was sittin' there it was because of him. You know, 'cause they could smell him?"

Smell him? Whether it was the words or a subliminal suggestion, Kash didn't know, but he suddenly had an urge to take a deep whiff of the air around him or, at the very least, smell his armpits. If he remembered one thing, he knew he'd put on deodorant today after he'd showered.

Marty let out a long groan, her face pained. "Lord love a duck. So they attacked?"

But Darnell shook his dark head. "Nuh-uh. Believe me, Boss, I was as surprised as anyone, 'cause this boy smelled good, and you know, at NOPE, there ain't always the code of honor we folks follow. Some don't resist temptation, if ya feel what I'm sayin'."

Code of honor? Temptation? Was this NOPE some kind of cult? No. That couldn't be. Cults didn't have codes of honor. They had followers who handed out pamphlets at the airport and wore flowers in their hair. So what code of honor did "we folks" follow, and who *was* "we folks"?

"So get to the point, D. What the fuck went down?" Nina groused, her coal-black eyes boring holes into Kash's face as she plopped down next to Darnell on the coffee table and patted his muscled thigh.

"I cain't say for sure who started what, but you know the boys who hang out there, don't ya? All sorts a scumbags—"

Wanda's finger shot up in the air, cutting Darnell off. She gave him a stern nun's gaze. "Why were *you* there, buddy? You're most definitely not a scumbag."

Darnell grinned. "'Cause they got the best dang crêpes Suzette I ever had. That Whitmore guy is a trained chef. You remember him, right? Tall, skinny. Dragon, I think."

There was a groan from another part of the room, followed by the sight of a short round elderly man with, of all things, blue hair. He was dressed in a bathrobe and fuzzy bear slippers.

Crepes... Yeah. Kash remembered vaguely seeing crepes and thinking how strange that was for such a dump.

"Master Darnell, how many times have I told you, I shall make you crêpes Suzette, if you wish. There's no need to go to that pox on humanity of a watering hole!"

Kash stared at the man with the stuffy British accent, who stuck his hand out to him and smiled, forgetting all about hearing the word *dragon*. "I'm Archibald, resident caretaker, cook, launderer, house cleaner, babysitter, surrogate grandfather for these fair maidens three, and their respective spouses and children. Oh, and of course all their clients. Lovely to meet you."

Kash found himself taking the man's hand in his—it was warm and soft and soothing—but he had no idea what he meant by client and he wasn't sure he wanted to.

Darnell grinned at the blue-haired man. "Look, Arch, you got a lot on your plate. I ain't puttin' more there."

"So you're telling me NOPE has crêpes Suzette? That's like saying Davio's—you know, that minimum two-hundred-dollars-a-plate Italian place over on

Westerfield?—has Big Macs," Wanda scoffed, smoothing her chestnut hair away from her face.

Darnell clucked his tongue. "I'm tellin' ya, Boss, there's a cordon bleu trained dragon who works there. Man knows his way 'round a stove and a crepe. It's like eatin' heaven wrapped up in euphoria."

Kash took a deep, deep breath. *You did not hear dragon used as a noun in conjunction with a cordon bleu trained chef, Kash Samuels. You did not.*

Nina flicked her fingers at Darnell, right under his nose. "Enough with the GD food I can't even fucking eat. Jesus, you lot are insensitive. Synthetic blood ain't a crepe, for shit's sake. Now, get on with this damn story. Waffles is gonna need to go potty soon and I got shit to do."

"Anyway, that's why I was there," Darnell explained, grabbing at Nina's fingers and tucking them into his meaty paw with a fond smile. "So Kash here, he came in, and like I said it got quiet, but not for the reason I was thinkin'. Y'all, the demons and the vampires are at it again."

Kash cocked his head, leaning forward to be sure he'd heard right.

"Aw, fuck. Was it the biker vamps? Those assholes need a good kick in the sac," Nina hissed. "I'm so sick of those raging fucks giving us a bad name."

Kash, despite all his misery, almost laughed. If anyone knew a raging fuck, Nina was likely your girl.

Darnell nodded once more, as if this was a

perfectly normal conversation. "I know how you feel, Boss. Those nuttier-than-squirrel-turd demons give the good guys like me a bad name, too."

Yup. He'd heard right. Demons and vampires. In fact, he quite suddenly remembered he'd heard the words vampire and ogre at the bar, too...

Jesus effin' Christ, these people were crackers. He needed to haul his sorry ass on outta here. Wherever here was. Yet, he couldn't find the will to move—or was he just afraid to move? He didn't want to startle the crazy with any sudden plays for the door.

"So a fight ensued, I'm guessing," Marty provided, pulling a throw pillow to her lap and folding her clasped hands over it.

Darnell ran a hand over his eyes, scrubbing them as though to wipe away a bad memory. "A fight like I ain't ever seen, and somehow, big boy here got all caught up in it. And listen, I tried to get to him fast as I could, but..."

Wanda sighed, leaning forward to give him a pat on his muscled thigh. "But there were too many, weren't there?"

His expression said resignation. "A-yup. I'm pretty fast, but I ain't that fast. So he got all in the middle of the mess, and you know how that goes when a buncha paranormals get to brawlin'."

How does that go? Kash wondered.

Nina cracked her knuckles while she eyed Kash. "So how many paranormals, do ya think? And what were they? They sure as shit weren't just vampires and demons, because he has pink hair that'd make our Esther jealous."

There were those words again. Vampire. Demon. Jesus, make the world stop. He wanted to get off. And who the hell was Esther?

"Nope. I can't remember 'em all, but I know for sure I saw a merman, a warlock, a buncha werewolves, a couple'a bears, and it seems the gargoyles ain't mad at a night out on the town, either. They were sluggin' back Jack like it was gonna be gone forever by daybreak. And I already mentioned the vampires and demons."

"Jesus and a bucket of chicken," Nina groaned, eyeballing him with more gusto. "Dude, you—are —fucked."

"Nina!" Marty yelped, swatting the space between them with her manicured red nails. "Don't say that to a client. As if he isn't already terrified, he doesn't need your pile-on. You're the worst, Queen of Darkness."

Nina threw up her middle finger as she rose from the coffee table. "Fuck off, Marty. We don't know how to deal with this shit. He *is* fucked. You know what this damn well means, right?"

Marty shrugged her shoulders. "Sort of..."

"He's already showing some signs of a merman and a werewolf by the looks of that raggedy-ass tail. But how much more fucked does it get if you're not one, not two, but *all the paranormal things*? That's what

I'd call fucked—as in, fuckity-fuck-fucked. You heard Darnell, he said bear, gargoyle, warlock, demon and who knows what else. All the things. He's every damn thing—like a melting pot of paranormal shit stew."

"I think there was a dragon, too," Darnell chirped.

Blinking, Kash didn't need to lean in for clarification this time. He'd heard *all the things*.

Vampire, demon, gargoyle, merman, warlock, werewolf, dragon and bear? Had he heard that right?

Had he missed any paranormal nouns?

Were there actually any left?

CHAPTER

THREE

"Oh, Mara, Harry, thank you for coming so late!" Marty said as two very good-looking, if not studious people entered the chaos that had become his life, standing in the middle of this charming living room in beige and white with, according to Wanda, a little moss green for a pop of color.

"Hah!" Nina crowed. "My favorite nerds are here!"

The woman named Mara, her long dark hair in a high pony that swung against the back of her puffy, red down vest, gave Marty a hard hug. "Of course we came. I don't know if we can help, but we're always here for you." She turned to the tall boy and opened her arms. "Carl, give me some love!"

Carl went into her arms with his crooked grin and stilted speech. "Glaaad...glad to see you."

Harry, a towering man with horn-rimmed glasses,

was the guy from some cosmetics company the women had been talking about while he remained unable to make himself move off the damn couch.

"Marty, good to see you!" he chimed in with a smile and a thump on the back for Carl.

Wanda was next, giving them each a warm hug. "We didn't know who else to call, but we're hoping you guys know someone in your field who might be able to...um, assist us?"

Harry nodded his dark head, peeling off his overcoat to reveal a sweater vest over a crisp white shirt and tie. "I think we might be able to help. There's a woman named Scotia McNealy—or Scotty, as she prefers—who's doing some really groundbreaking work with mixed-paras. Her parents are of the McKissick clan in Scotland."

Nina thumped Harry on the back and smiled up at him, and even in his stupor, Kash couldn't help but think that if she was beautiful when she was scowling, Nina was freakishly flawless when she smiled. "You mean that tyrant Orgon McKissick? He's a total fuck. Hate him."

Harry grinned down at her. "I'd expect nothing less from you, Keeper of the Crypt. And yes, that's exactly who I mean. Now, your contempt for Orgon McKissick aside, how's my man Carl? Charlie and Greg? And your newest addition, Waffles?"

Were these people—people who talked of demons and vampires and Scottish clans—really all just standing around, having a conversation about children and waffles as if it was normal to use those words in the same sentence?

What the fuck was happening?

Nina winked, her thick lashes sweeping her cheek. "Everybody's real good. Real fuckin' good. And yours? What are those little devils up to these days?"

"They're not so little anymore. Fletch is scoping colleges for next year and Mimi is killing us with her teenage angst."

Nina barked a laugh, leaving Kash in awe. *She laughed.* As in, had a joyous response. Kash didn't know whether he was coming or going.

"And how's Donna? I can't believe she's almost six now. Christ, time flies, doesn't it, Ass-Sniffer?"

Kash blinked. She'd called this hulk of a man an ass-sniffer and he hadn't even batted an eye. Nay. In fact, he laughed.

Kash didn't think he had any more what-the-fucks left in him, but...*what the fuck?*

"Donna's amazing. Growing like a weed, doing really great in first grade." He held up his large hand and grinned. "We had a nail-painting party the other day and she chose orange in honor of my sister."

Nina gave him a wistful look, one that made Kash pause. "You guys still honoring Donna's memory?"

Harry nodded, his throat working as he swallowed. "Not as often as we used to. Time has healed the urgency and frequency of those meetings, but we never miss her birthday or holidays, and we always tell our Donna we named her after the greatest sister her dad could have asked for."

Nina bowed her head for a brief moment, as if in reverence. Carl, too, nodded his head in acknowledgement.

When Nina looked up, Kash saw her eyes had gone warm. "Those kids are damn lucky to have you two. Damn lucky, indeed." Giving Harry a quick hug, she said in a husky tone that sounded to Kash like it was filled with emotion, "You tell Fletch, no matter how big he gets, he'll always be my favorite little man to watch Sponge-Bob with. And tell my girl Mimi she owes me a trip to the pet store. We'll get Miss Coconut some goodies."

Harry gripped Nina's hand, his eyes meeting hers briefly, and that was the moment when, even amidst the turmoil his body was experiencing, Kash understood these people had gone through something. Some kind of trauma, and they'd bonded in a way that didn't need words.

"You bet I will, Crypt Keeper. Now, on to the immediate problem. As I said, Mara knows someone who might at least be able to pinpoint what he is, or maybe I should say, how many species Kash is."

Well, that was just about enough of that. *Species?* Now he was a new species? It wasn't enough that they used words like clan and paranormal and dragon and merman, but to be classified as a species other than human?

He wanted out. *Now.*

Using every last ounce of energy he had, his legs shaking, his fin flapping, his bushy tail bobbing, his head throbbing and his blood rushing to parts unknown in his body, he pushed himself off the cushiony couch and stood for the first time in what felt like hours.

Clearing his throat, a throat that felt raw and tight, Kash Samuels took control the way he always did.

Well, mostly. He was a little stumbling, a little awkward, and damn, his tail was more of a hinderance than one might expect, but control was what he was after. Pushing his way into the crowd of people in this gorgeous living room, filled with beautiful rustic furniture and soft, comfortable seating, Kash Samuels made his stand.

"Look, I don't know what the hell is going on here," he croaked, and to his ears, his voice sounded weak and wobbly, but that wasn't going to stop him. "But I'm going the hell home. I'm not gonna listen to another word about vampires and werewolves and mer-fucking-men. That's not even a thing, for Christ's sake! I don't know what you people believe in, but it's not my flex. It's crazy. That's what it is. And I'm not going to see anyone so we can *identify* my species. Are we clear?"

DAKOTA CASSIDY

He'd startled them. That much was evident when everyone stopped talking and gaped at him.

In the midst of the uncomfortable silence, quite suddenly, Nina threw her head back and laughed. The cackle erupted from her throat like oil from a well.

"What's so damn funny?" he barked, knowing he was being incredibly rude to these people who hadn't actually harmed him. Who had, in fact, given him a warm place to sit while he recuperated from a bar fight he didn't remember.

They weren't bad people. They were just insane people.

Wanda grabbed Nina just before she latched onto his throat, but that didn't stop her mouth from moving as she fought against Wanda's grip. "You wanna know what's so damn funny, you dick-knuckle?"

Did he want to know? From the look on Nina's perfect face, survey said, no. She was infuriated. He knew due to the flare of her nostrils and the narrowing of her blacker-than-black eyes.

Kash shrank backward with a wince, all his bravado lying somewhere by his feet on the hardwood floor.

Gulping, he tried lifting his chin to appear as if his dignity hadn't evaporated, but ended up meekly asking on a gulp, "What's so funny, *Crypt Keeper*?"

Of all that was holy, had he let that pet name, one clearly reserved for Harry and Nina, slip from his lips?

Yep. Slipped right from his big yap like hot melted caramel over cold ice cream.

Harry snorted so hard, it echoed around the large space, but Mara nudged him in the ribs and hissed, "Have you lost your mind? How long have you been a part of this family? She's going to make a bowtie for your neck out of your intestines if you don't zip it, *honey*."

Instantly, Harry straightened, as if suddenly remembering he was tangling with the angriest woman on the planet and cleared his throat, adjusting his sweater vest. "Sorry," he mumbled sheepishly.

"Here's what's so funny, Kash," Marty held up a compact mirror, her expression bland as though she'd been there, done that. "Look over your left shoulder."

So he looked.

First, he took a breath so deep, his eyeballs rolled to the back of his head and his chest burned.

Then he blinked.

Next, his mouth fell open. Literally, the lower half of his jaw unhinged itself as he stared at his reflection in the small mirror.

"Is that..." He couldn't even finish the question. How did you ask a question like that without sounding stark-raving mad?

Someone flicked the ends of his hair and whispered near his ear, "Uh-huh. Not sure if it's angel or fuckin' dragon. We gotta let it grow more before we can make a clear diagnosis. Ain't that right, girls?"

Nina. Of course it was Nina in his ear, reveling in his chaotic pain.

Horror coursed through his veins. He had a wing. A *wing*.

Gulping, he asked, "But...how...?"

Nina cackled in delight. "Because you're not just an accidental fucking paranormal. You're a *shitload* of accidents. Or Accidental AF. Whichever you prefer." Then she slapped him on the back.

It was the last thing he felt before a vise grip took hold of him and began twisting his muscles into knots.

As he fell to the floor, his body convulsing and pandemonium ensuing around him, Kash thought about what he'd seen in that mirror, and he crossed his fingers.

If, in all this absolute madness, he could pick what kind of wings he was bestowed? It damn well better be dragon wings, or his brother was never going to let him live it down.

CHAPTER

FOUR

"Kash? Can you open your eyes for me?"

A soft hand touched his arm, squeezing his wrist and checking his pulse. The scent of antiseptic and a musky-floral perfume assaulted his nose.

"Kash?" the sweet voice called again. "Can you open your eyes, please?"

As everything that happened came rushing back to him, Kash decided no. No, he wasn't going to open his eyes. He liked them closed where he couldn't see what new horror had befallen him next.

It was enough to see the fin poking out of his leg and the long strand of pink hair growing from his scalp. He was good.

Machines beeped around him, and the narrowness of the mattress on either side of his hips indicated a hospital bed—which likely meant they'd gotten in

33

touch with the person the nerdy but beautiful couple had been talking about and he was in a lab somewhere.

The description of the person they claimed could help bolted into his brain. A scientist who was making progress working with *mixed-paranormals*—or something like that.

Kash fought the stiffening of his body as he put that sentence together in a summarization of his predicament. If he were a betting man, he'd bet this *scientist* was going to use him as some sort of lab rat.

Probably much the way the government would were the situation reversed and they had found a mixed-paranormal.

Which meant he needed to keep his eyes closed.

Someone leaned over him, right across his waist, someone who smelled distinctly like Irish Spring soap and something else he couldn't identify.

"He's playin' possum. I can smell it," a husky voice announced, giving him a hard poke in the arm.

"Possum," a voice agreed slowly. If he remembered correctly, it was Carl. The sweet-looking boy who had green skin and duct tape on his middle finger.

The husky voice was Nina's. If he remembered nothing else about this night, he'd remember her voice and the gleeful way she enjoyed bringing down the hammer of pain.

"Nina, back away from the man and let him have

some air." That was Marty, always ready to scold her friend with as much glee as Nina took in taunting him.

"Look, Blondie, do you want to figure this the fuck out or don't you? He needs to be awake so Whatsher-name can run tests or whatever the hell she's gonna do. We can't help him if he's gonna play candy-ass and pretend he's not awake."

"It's Scotty. Scotty McNealy. *Dr. Scotia McNealy*, to be precise," that sweet voice corrected.

There was a rustle, possibly feet scuffling, and then Nina's angry voice. "I don't give a fuck if you're the new Doctor Who. He's bullshittin' you and I don't have time for bullshit. I got a kid, and a dog, and a husband I wanna go home to. Now open your damn eyes, lab rat, and open 'em *now*."

Kash almost chuckled. Oh, Nina-zilla. She was so much sunshine.

"Nina?" Wanda admonished. "Please refrain from calling him a lab rat. Not only is it rude, but it's not true. No one wants to conduct tests on him that aren't necessary for anything other than his greater good in his new paranormal world. Scotty...er...Dr. McNealy said we need to find out how to control his shifts. You did see what I saw back at my house, didn't you?"

Nina let out a long snort. "You're not fucking seri-ous, are you? I took fucking pictures of his ass flopping around the floor like a fish outta water. Never saw so many damn paranormals in one body at one time.

Didja see his bear paw? I think I got a pic of it. It was the size of a farkin' side of beef."

His insides froze. Last count, he had a fin, a tail, and the tip of a wing.

Don't forget your pink hair.

Right. Now there was a bear paw involved?

Was this even real?

Someone cleared their throat and spoke in a voice he didn't recognize, but it was even and pleasant to his ears. "Ladies, I think it's best we stop talking about him as though he's not here."

"Well, I wouldn't have to do that if the motherfucker would open his damn eyes and stop being a pussy, would I?"

Nina could call him all the names she liked to egg him on. He wasn't opening his eyes. He wasn't ready. Plus, he feared opening his eyes would hurt as much as the rest of him did, and he didn't want that either.

His head was about to burst wide open and his muscles felt like they could explode at any moment. Whatever had happened back at Wanda's house, it sure as fuck hadn't been good—because every inch of him ached.

A hand came to rest on his forearm. "Kash, I'll give you something for the pain if you'll open your eyes and tell me where it hurts. I can't see anything outwardly physical other than your new appendages, so you'll have to help me out in order for me to assess your condition."

Appendages? Christ almighty.

He swallowed hard, the lump in his throat growing. "Why do my eyes have to be open to tell you that? Last time I checked, all I needed was my mouth."

There was a small sigh, then what he thought was a smile in her voice when she said softly, "There you are."

"Where am I?"

Kash peeked around with half an open eye, noting there were no windows in the room, but there were plenty of tables made of shiny steel, holding microscopes and one of those spinny things he'd seen forensic shows use for vials of blood.

"You're in the basement labs of Bobbie-Sue Cosmetics."

He clenched his fists. Bobbie-Sue? The makeup? He'd had a girlfriend once who swore by their makeup and something called a color wheel. She'd been a summer, if he recalled correctly.

Was the company some sort of front for nefarious testing? Were all those commercials and endcaps at stores just a ruse for whatever was going on behind the scenes? It was a makeup company...makeup companies tested on animals all the time.

That infuriated him, especially thinking of his own dog, Janet, part pit bull, part Great Dane. He'd adopted her from the Humane Society only moments before she was due for euthanasia, and he couldn't imagine his life without all sixty-pounds of her goofy love.

Thankfully, she was safe in doggie daycare for now.

Shit. He slammed his eyes shut again, hoping to at least quash one bit of the sensory overload he was experiencing.

"I know what you're thinking, and it's not that at all," the doctor said, obviously reading his thoughts. "Marty was gracious enough to loan me some space so I can try and figure out how to help you. And I promise, I only want to help. No forced chemical exposure or toxicity testing for you, my friend. None."

Then she chuckled at a joke he didn't get. A nerd joke, he assumed.

Marty—he guessed, by the scent of her perfume— sat on the edge of his bed and patted his leg. "Scotty's right. We don't test our products on animals. Forced chemical exposure is a test used on animals in labs."

"That's a pretty specific bit of knowledge," he commented, the words loaded with sarcasm.

Through his half-open eye, he saw Marty's face go dark and, he had to admit, he wasn't a fan of her displeasure. "I own Bobbie-Sue, good sir. I make it my business, no matter how horrifying it can be, to know everything I need to know about testing cosmetics. I know what goes on in every square inch of this place and I can assure you, I'd die before I'd allow any kind of animal testing. *Ever.*"

But what about human testing—or whatever he was now?

"Kash Samuels," Wanda said. Nay, demanded. "Open your eyes *this instant*. There are people here who've taken time out of their lives to help you. Most especially Scotty, who dropped everything to be here, and believe me, you're going to need her help. Now, please open your eyes, or I'll open them for you and at best, you'll find that mightily unpleasant."

It was one thing to have Nina-zilla mad at him. She obviously lived to sow fear and discord. But Wanda? Not warm, welcoming Wanda.

Even if the plan was to experiment on him, on a scale of one to ten, he still liked Wanda the best so far, with Marty and Darnell as close seconds. She was a solid eight in the category of most hospitable.

Whoa, whoa, whoa. Was he rating his captors? Relating to them?

Did Stockholm syndrome come with being paranormal, too?

FIVE

*S*cotty McNealy looked down at the poor subject's...er, man's face and pursed her lips, waiting to see if he'd respond to Wanda's threat.

When he did, she was taken aback by the beauty of the color of his eyes, unsure if they were amber because of his new paranormal status or if they were normally the color of dark whiskey.

He stared at her for what felt like forever, and all her don't-get-too-personal training went right out the window.

He was the cutest lab rat she'd ever seen.

Drop-dead hot from head to toe.

Dark-haired, lean but muscled, smelled like fresh ocean air, biceps with just enough bulge to look like a place a girl could rest her head, and long legs with a sprinkling of hair poking through the holes in his jeans, holes he'd probably acquired from the fight he'd been in at NOPE.

And he was in one helluva pickle.

Nina the Terrible, who lived up to her reputation in the paranormal world, eyeballed her with those gorgeous dark eyes of hers.

Scotty knew of the three women. Who didn't? They were legends in the community. But actually meeting Nina and having her do all the things she was famous for, like cussing and threatening? That turned out to be larger than life, and she wasn't sure if she was awed or terrified.

Either way, she needed to get her spine right with the Lord and behave like the professional they'd hired.

Nina nudged Scotty. "Can we get the fuck on with this?"

Could she?

She didn't know what to do with this man. She had not a clue. He'd been shifting into one form or another at the speed of light before she'd stabilized him with a sedative. She'd never dealt with something like this before.

But she was determined to understand it because maybe it could help her...

As if he was suddenly truly seeing her, he said in a whiskey-soaked voice, "You're in a wheelchair."

Scotty grinned at him and used her sarcasm as her shield. "See what opening your eyes did for you? It helped you state the obvious."

Instantly, those pretty eyes went apologetic, as most did when they realized they'd pointed out said obvious. "Shit... I mean, shoot. I'm sorry. I think my manners are still back in that bar somewhere. I didn't mean to insult..."

She grinned harder because that's what she did— she deflected. "No worries. I'm not insulted. There's nothing insulting about having a wheelchair. People comment on it all the time. And as an FYI, I don't always need the wheelchair. I can walk." When Kash looked at her in question, she waved a hand at him. "It's a long, boring story. But I don't use the wheelchair unless I need to, and today I needed to because it's been a long day."

"People say shit to you about your wheelchair?" Nina mumbled, her tone filled with disgust. "I swear, the world is full of assholes."

Looking to Nina, Scotty still didn't know whether to be afraid or awed. She swallowed hard. What happened to her happened, and she'd dealt with it. It was just part of her life. "Sometimes."

"If that shit ever goes down and I'm around, I will fuck them up. You hear me? Like a nuclear bomb's gonna be less abrasive after I open up a can of whoop-ass."

Scotty was so busy trying to decide between being flattered and horrified, she almost didn't hear Marty say, "Nina has a dog named Waffles who's special needs. Our Mistress of the Dark is very sensitive—

especially if someone states the obvious. Aren't you, Bloodsucker?"

"Well, duh, Ass-Sniffer. Unless they're kids, who *should* fucking ask questions so as adults, they can learn *not* to ask stupid questions, it's a stupid fucking question."

Now Kash looked like he felt sorry for her, and Scotty hated that. "Can I start over?" he asked, and he was so stupid-cute, she couldn't have said no even if she'd wanted to.

She stuck out her hand. "Sure. I'm Dr. Scotia McNealy, or as most call me, Scotty. I have a bachelor's degree in biology/genetics and one in biophysics, and a Ph.D. in paranormal science and the study of all things supernaturally occurring, and I've been hired to help you. I *want* to help you."

While I try to help myself.

Now Kash really gave her a once-over as he shook her hand. "All of that and you're maybe, what? All of twenty-five?"

She winked and took her hand back, putting her fingers on the wheels of her chair. "Aren't you a flatterer? I'm thirty-seven and I've spent most of my life dedicated to studying paranormals."

He licked his lips as though he were afraid to ask the next question. Then he bit the inside of his cheek and clearly decided to ask anyway. "So what are you?"

She cocked her head and played stupid because it was funny. And because she hated that question almost as much as the one about her wheelchair. "What am I what?"

"What kind of paranormal are you?" Judging by the look on his face, Kash appeared as though he couldn't even fathom a circumstance where he'd have to ask such a question—yet, here he was, asking.

As a by the by, she wasn't any kind of anything. If only. She was an anomaly. A human, born by some bizarre twist of fate, to two vampires who never let her forget she was a human and all the flaws that came with it.

She deflected once more. She must keep this and all further interactions professional. If she'd learned anything, she'd learned to never get involved with a patient. The one time she had...

Suffice it to say, it had been bad. Very bad.

"We can talk about that later. Right now, how about you tell me your name, age, weight, the particulars. Also, any serious illnesses, surgeries?"

"Kash Samuels, hamburger flipper; forty; about two-fifty and six-four. No serious illnesses, no surgeries, no allergies."

Scotty popped her lips and nodded, tamping down a smile about his hamburger flipping. "What do you do for work, Kash?"

"I'm semi-retired."

Impressive. "At forty? Nice gig if you can get it." Whatever he actually did for a living, he probably wouldn't be able to return to it for a while. Not looking like this...

He grinned then, a beautiful, white-toothed grin that left deep grooves on either side of his full-ish mouth and canceled out all of the kooky things happening to his body. "I own a chain of burger joints called Brother's Burgers."

From the corner of the room, Marty and Wanda gasped. "You own Brother's Burgers? Best bacon avocado burger on sourdough I've ever had!" Wanda cooed, clapping her hands.

"And those crinkle fries? The truffle oil ones?" Marty raved and fanned herself. "Phew. Heaven and the Pearly Gates. One of my favorite guilty pleasures."

He nodded his acknowledgement in their direction. "I'm glad to hear that. My brother and I worked hard to build our brand."

"I think it's so cool that you own a restaurant," Marty said. "What brought that about?"

He shrugged. "It started as just a joke because as single bachelors living together, we ate a lot of fast-food burgers. Thin, flimsy soy patties with little to no flavor. I love to cook. We both do. It's kind of our thing, but we worked a lot, so we didn't have a lot of time to make meals and our shifts never aligned. One day, when we had a rare day off together, we were just messing around and I whipped up a hamburger patty that turned out pretty good. One thing led to another and we found our niche."

She was less interested in the burgers and more interested in how he'd lit up at the mention of his restaurant. He'd relaxed a little.

"So you do have family then?" Scotty asked. That could present a problem.

"I have my brother. No one else," Kash said, then focused across the room at the far wall.

Nina's eyes narrowed as she crossed her arms over her chest. "Is he gonna come lookin' for you? We don't need that kind of fucking trouble so early in the game. We gotta get shit right with you before you go telling the world."

Wincing, Kash cleared his throat. "Garrick's in Germany right now. We're looking to branch out with BB overseas. He'll be gone for at least the next month."

The look that washed over his face said he was worried. As though suddenly, he realized he was very alone. She'd lay bets it was because he thought no one would look for him, and if the evil plan were truly to turn him into their guinea pig, he'd end up on a missing persons list in some police precinct.

While she totally planned to run tests on him, there would be nothing diabolical. Not really...

Scotty tapped his hand with a finger, trying to be sensitive without getting too familiar. "You can call your brother, if you like. I don't know where your phone got to, but if it'll help to hear a familiar voice, we'll figure out what to tell him. You wouldn't be the first person to be accidentally turned into a paranormal. I'm sure the ladies of OOPS know how to break it to a family member, don't you, ladies?"

Kash frowned, and yep—even then, he was still easy on the eye. "OOPS?" He stuttered the acronym.

Nina rolled her eyes as if explaining were akin to doing a thousand sit-ups on a full stomach. "Out in the Open Paranormal Support. Get it?" she crowed. "You know, like, 'oops. There was an accident and I got the shit beat out of me in a bar and now I'm fucked, but these three broads know what the shit they're talking about when they say they can help'? That kind of OOPS. Funny, right?"

"A gas," he said, his tone wooden.

Still, Kash relaxed just a bit, or as much as she supposed he could with half a wing poking out of his back. She still wasn't sure if it was dragon or angel or anything at all—it was too early in its stages of growth to tell.

"We do this all the time, Kash," Wanda explained. "I mean, not exactly this...er, not with as many accidents at once like you've had. But we've helped easily a hundred clients or more. In fact, we were once accidents, too."

He appeared to really like Wanda, because he gave her a thin smile. "This happened to you, too?"

"Sort of. We'll explain another time. Maybe after you've rested. Anyway, we'd be happy to talk to your brother with you, if you'd like," Marty offered with a warm smile.

He winced when he shifted positions on the bed, the rough sheets rasping against his skin. "I just talked to him last night, so if you're worried he's going to come looking for me, he won't. At least not for a little while. There are too many women in Germany to chase, but thanks all the same."

Two bright spots burned her cheeks, and Kash noticed. "TMI?"

Scotty stayed silent, remembering her promise to herself to remain removed.

He shrugged his wide shoulders. "Sorry. It's just the truth. Garrick's a little bit of a dog."

Scotty shook her head, looking at her feet before she settled her gaze on him. "I'm not worried about your brother showing up. But you'll have some explaining to do, and right now, I don't think you're in any shape to do anything but recuperate from that frenzy of shifts. It's clearly taken a toll. You're as pale as freshly fallen snow."

"Probably 'cause he's vampire on top of all the other shit he's got goin' on. Ain't that right, pretty boy? Your fangs are gonna be the shit, though, with your teeth lookin' like a Colgate commercial and all." Nina smiled at him, once more taking obvious delight in his pain.

Marty came to stand next to Nina, pinching her arm with two manicured fingers. "We don't know if he's vampire, too, Nina. Shut your trap, would you? Let

Scotty determine what he is before we draw conclusions."

Scotty smiled her best reassuring smile. "On that note, let's talk about your levels of pain, yes?"

"I feel like someone pulled me through a damn keyhole. Is that a level?"

Wanda chuckled in sympathy, her laughter light and airy as she tweaked his toe. "If it's not, it should be."

Scotty nodded. So she'd heard. She'd dealt with subjects who'd been accidentally turned, but no one in recent centuries—though, she knew they existed because of these women and the stories surrounding their support group.

In her research, she'd run across and interviewed tons of people who'd been bitten or scratched as far back as the sixteen-hundreds. None of those cases helped her, and when she began looking in earnest, she'd come across very few paranormals with an origin story of being *born* paranormal.

Still, she'd give her right arm to be one of those few.

Straightening, Scotty decided Kash needed a night of rest before they went any further. A good, stiff tranquilizer should help with that. This way, while he rested up, she could wrap her head around his case, figure out what combination of paranormal he was, and process what to do next.

"Dr. McNealy?" Trina Sutter, her new lab assistant,

popped open the door to the lab and poked her pretty dark head inside. Everyone turned to look at her. Trina grinned in response and waggled her fingers in greeting. "Hey, y'all!"

Scotty sighed. If Trina asked her one more time when her shift would be over so she could go home because she had a date, Scotty was going to set Nina loose on her.

Backing away from the bed, she introduced her wayward employee. "Everyone, this is Trina Sutter. My lab assistant."

"*Head* lab assistant," Trina corrected cheerfully, pointing to the tag with her name on it, the one she insisted be made for her lab coat.

"I only have one, Trina," Scotty reminded her, remembering to keep her words soft-ish and ignoring the impulse to throttle her.

Trina was a lot. A huge handful of almost zero help at all. She'd flunked out of college, but her father, a prominent physician, was friends with Scotty's father who was in finance, so he'd called in a favor.

It was enough that she'd agreed to help out her father's friend and to keep her resentment in check over the fact that Trina was paranormal. Fae, to be precise, cute rainbow-colored wings and all. Her paranormalness wasn't her fault and much like any kind of discrimination, Scotty recognized her anger for what it was—her own insecurity.

But to find Trina was almost useless? Well, that was too much.

Trina's wings fluttered, meaning she didn't like being corrected. "Right. Well, whatever. Listen, your dad's on the phone. You want me to tell him you're busy?"

Ugh. Banner McNealy's phone calls meant only one thing—he was checking up on her. She could almost hear him now. *"Make sure you do me proud, Princess."*

What that really meant was: Don't screw up with the OOPS ladies. They're very important people in our community and a good connection to have. Don't embarrass us with your fumbling humanness.

Sighing, Scotty nodded her head. "Nothing's changed since I asked you to tell him that the last time he called, Trina."

She clucked her tongue and planted a hand on her slender hip. "I'm just checking. You know how he can be."

Did she ever.

Boy, did she ever.

SIX

K ash listened with his whole being. Not that he had much of a choice; he could hear *everything*. In fact, he was pretty sure he heard some poor guy flipping the pages of a magazine as he made use of the facilities in North Dakota.

Still, he leaned an ear toward the lab door as the voices of the women drifted away until there was nothing but the sound of his heart monitor—which, ironically, had the strangest sluggish beats he'd ever heard. One minute, it was like someone was playing the bongos in his chest. The next, there was almost nothing.

All of which the very attractive Scotty had assured him was normal for someone in his predicament. And she *was* attractive. Petite as the day was long, with chestnut-brown hair to the middle of her back, partially clamped in a clip on top of her head that looked like the ones he used to keep his chip bags closed.

Big green eyes and long sweeping lashes sat in her heart-shaped face, with raspberry-colored lips that looked as soft as pillows completed Dr. Scotty's picture.

She'd assured him that his heart, as well as all of his other organs, were bound to be erratic due to the changes his body was going through.

Sure, sure, sure. He'd sat in this bed and listened to all the kooky theories these women had about the changes happening to him. And of course, he saw the changes in his body, too.

He did have eyes—eyes that could read the tiny writing on a medicine bottle on one of the tables, easily ten feet away. Which was weird, but whatever. He was almost positive everything could be explained by a plain old human doctor.

Maybe the unruly hair—which had doubled in thickness on his head and was growing in weird patches on his arms—and the tail were hypertrichosis. Maybe all the other things happening to him were also medically explained anomalies.

What these nuts hadn't considered was that he watched TV. Yes-siree. He'd seen plenty of weird diseases on the Discovery Channel, on a show that had played on a loop when he was laid up with the flu a couple of years ago.

God, he didn't think anything could have been as

bad as that had been. Aches, fever, pain in his joints—even his eyelashes had hurt. However, it was nothing compared to how he felt right now.

It didn't mean he was a werewolf or a merman or a bear or any of the things these women had determined were his ailments.

And he didn't care what the cute Dr. Scotty said. She eyed him like a rare steak. He'd heard them talking in the hall, and that she hadn't shared with him that she was human, too, left him mightily suspicious.

How had a human woman—a doctor with a bazillion degrees, no less—landed here, with all the quote-unquote *paranormals*? How and why?

Bottom line? He was almost positive she planned to conduct tests on him that he couldn't be certain weren't unsavory. It was the only explanation. She was in cahoots with the rest of these people. To what end, he didn't know.

Maybe they really did believe in the supernatural. Maybe they believed vampires and mermaids existed. David Koresh had convinced people he was the final Branch Davidian prophet. People drank the Kool-Aid all the time.

Maybe they really did think what was happening to him could be attributed to being paranormal, but that was, for all intents and purposes, insane.

But what about Nina's fangs, Kash? You saw them, remember? And that lab assistant? She had wings, buddy. Wings!

That did niggle him a bit, but then he told his inner self to shut the hell up and stop making a case for these kooks. They might appear harmless enough— well, except for Nina—but cults all came across as a bunch of tree huggers until they weren't.

Kash wasn't going to let them turn him into some kind of sacrifice.

No can do. He was getting the hell out of Dodge, ASAP, despite the fact that he felt like complete dog shit. He could feel that way at the nearest hospital— with other humans.

Okay, so explain how she picked your over-two-hundred-pound ass up off the floor with one hand and didn't even grunt. Go ahead. I'll wait.

Shut. Up.

The time for playing around had come and gone. No more doubting himself. He was out.

Wincing, Kash looked down at his arm and instantly went dizzy. He hated needles. *Hated them.* The very thought of them made him want to yack up his lunch, but he didn't have a choice if he wanted to bust out of here. He had to stop the tranquilizer from dripping into his veins and the only way to do that was to pull the plug.

Planting a hand on his forearm, Kash plucked the needle out and fought his revulsion, covering his mouth when he gagged. Throwing it to the ground, he could only hope he'd stopped the drip of drugs quickly enough to keep his wits about him.

As he threw his legs over the side of the bed and stood up, ignoring the fin sprouting from his ankle and the ache in his back from the horror protruding from his spine, he decided so far so good.

Soon, he'd have some answers to his questions that didn't have solutions like, maybe you're a vampire.

Hah!

And whoa. Kash gripped the side of the bed until the dizzy spell passed. Gritting his teeth, he crept toward the door and listened some more.

All was quiet on the western front. But what was beyond the door? There was no window to peek out. No way to tell for sure there wasn't someone right outside the gray steel door of the lab.

Balls to the wall, buddy. It's either make a run for it or be someone's test monkey.

Squaring his shoulders, Kash nudged the door open and looked around. There wasn't much to see. A chair by the door, a small desk with nothing on it but a closed laptop, and lots of other doors. Though, his suddenly Bionic Man eyesight came in handy.

He saw all the way down to the end of the long, white-tiled corridor. In fact, he saw every scuff mark on the floor—the floor at the *end* of the hallway, and the dent in the trim above the tile.

Okay, that was radically crazy, but he didn't have time to research his mind's database for a medical explanation. He had to make a break for it.

Without another thought, Kash bolted out the door, the cool air hitting the torn spots of his jeans as everything passed his eyes in a blur.

And suddenly, he was at the end of the hallway. He knew in that second it was stupid to stop and ponder how quickly he'd gotten here and how his feet nearly took flight, but damn.

Damn.

Inhaling a deep breath, he pushed open the door. Thankfully it wasn't locked, but that didn't mean they weren't trying to contain him. They thought he was drugged, however, which worked to his advantage.

Outside the door was another long hall with even more hallways, but with this crazy ability to see clear into next year, he managed to identify a door marked "exit" at the far end of one passage, and headed straight for it, ignoring the sharp stab of pain in his back and the growing thickness of his tongue.

Whatever that was on his back, he hoped the plastic surgeon he intended to consult had a chainsaw big enough to get it off him. Though, it was probably going to leave a hellacious scar.

But zero time for vanity now. Kash pushed through the exit door and found himself at the entrance to the labs, staring at another exit across the room. If he was on the right track, he'd be in the parking lot in no time.

Praying he didn't set off an alarm, Kash held his breath and barreled through the door.

Just as he was taking a deep breath of bitter-cold

air he didn't feel at all, while surveying what was, indeed, a nearly empty parking lot, he felt an iron grip on his shoulder that painfully jarred his back protrusion and made him wobble, followed by yet another dizzy spell.

"Sweet baby Jesus and a hot wing, are you insane, motherfucker? Get back in that damn bed!"

Nina-zilla.

Eek.

Kash stopped thinking then and reacted. He didn't consider what would happen if Nina caught up with him. He didn't think about what they might do to him in retaliation. He didn't even think about how sluggish he was beginning to feel.

He just ran—hard, far—with the cackle of his nemesis in his ears as she shouted, "We got a runner, girls!"

At those words, out of the blue, he was an Olympic gold medalist, taking off toward the woods, where he saw every knot in every tree, every ice-coated branch with an eerie magnification.

He dove into the forest, not even stopping to acknowledge that he'd made it to the edge of the thick trees faster than The Flash, but he did remember to be a little impressed by how cool that was. The twelve-tear-old geek in him was giddy.

Don't be such a nerdy dork, Kash.

But do run.

And that's exactly what he did. He tried to block out the stomp of feet behind him, the cries of the women as they tried to stop him with pretty lies like "we only want to help!" and ran, his feet almost feeling like they belonged to someone else.

Blurs of white trees and logs covered in snow flit past him as he pumped his aching legs harder, faster, running aimlessly without thought to where he was going.

He didn't know where the hell he was anyway, but he did know he needed to get real medical help. Snow crunched under his feet—feet he only just realized had no shoes, but that didn't stop him.

Never once finding himself out of breath—which was bananas, it was as if he had endless energy despite how terrible he felt—Kash kept running

Until he was knocked over by a brick wall, that is. Sacked face first into the crunchy landscape like a lump of bones and flesh.

He hit the hard, snow-covered ground with a thunk so loud, it echoed obnoxiously throughout the forest. A large foot came to rest at the back of his neck and a gruff male voice yelled, "Got him!"

Kash struggled. Of course he did. He wasn't ready to give up his man card yet. But to no avail. Whoever had their foot on his neck was planted quite firmly and there was no removing it.

"Chiiill, Colgate Commercial," Nina crowed with a

sharp glare. She got down on all fours and flicked the pink strands of his hair sprawled on the ground. "We're just trying to help you, fucknuts, and it really kinda pisses me off that you have me out here in the middle of the GD night, chasing after you like you're some flippin' wild animal who just escaped the pound. Don't be so bloody ungrateful."

Ooo. She was big mad.

But help was the last thing they were offering.

"Could you please ask whoever's got their foot on my neck to remove it?" he gritted out, his lips pressed to the cold ground, his tongue becoming uncooperative.

"Sorren!" Wanda called out, just as Marty slid into him like he was second base.

"Oomph!" she squealed, rolling to his side with a grunt. With an exasperated sigh, Marty narrowed her eyes as they lie almost nose to nose. "Damnit, Nina, could you give me a head's up next time? You know I can't slow down when I'm in full run. And would you just look! I think I broke a nail in the fall." She held up her small hand, letting her fingers flash under the bright moon.

Nina laughed and sat back on her haunches; her face paler than pale under the black night filled with stars. "Nah. That's no fun. Know what *is* fun? When you trip and fall. That's funny as fuck."

Marty growled her displeasure before she turned

her neck and angled her gaze at him. "You okay, Kash?"

Kash was, in fact, not okay. "Aside from the concrete foot on my neck and the fact that the people who claim they're trying to *help* me are members of some kooky cult, I'm outstanding."

All the women began to laugh—snorts and all.

Marty clapped his back as she sat up. "We're not a cult, ding-dong, and I think it's time we prove it to you."

Before Marty could continue, the foot on his neck moved and Kash instantly rolled over to stare up into the eyes of a man the size of a mountain. He had his arms crossed over his wide chest and a look of displeasure on his craggy, worn face.

Wanda tapped his arm with her fingers and gave him a warm smile. "Sorren, what brings you here?"

"Him," the mountain grunted with a point of his finger, making a face of displeasure. "One of mine bit him at NOPE."

Wanda nodded, crossing her ankles together, her feet clad in sensible but sophisticated black heels. "So you want to claim his as yours? Is that why you're here?"

Wait. *What?*

Claim him? He wasn't a piece of property to be claimed like he was in the lost and found box at the local church, but somehow, the presence of this hulk of a man kept him from speaking up. If he went around "claiming" people, who knew what else he was capable of.

Sorren puffed out a cloud of breath. "It's the right thing to do, Wanda. I always take responsibility for my pack—especially when that fucker...er, screw-up Hanson's involved. He just can't stay the hell out of trouble, but he really did it this time, didn't he?"

Kash, finally finding his voice, scrambled to his feet, nearly losing his footing on the icy ground, he stood up so fast. "No one's claiming anything. I don't know who the hell you and your *pack* are, whatever that means, but I don't want anything to do with your kind of insanity. Now, if you'll 'scuse me, I'm gonna keep running away from you flaming kooks. Have a great night." His words were slurring, but regardless, he thought he'd effectively made his point.

However, Kash didn't even take a step before Nina was in front of him in a flash—literally—blocking him from going forward. "No can do, buddy. You can't be out there runnin' loose with your half-ass wing and those flappy lips while you're on drugs. You're gonna get hurt, and I can't let that happen. Not on my watch. I'll slaughter your ass before I let that happen."

Wanda was beside her in a matter of a nanosecond, her pretty face as serene as ever. "Nina, don't threaten. Kash is afraid and uncertain and he has every right to be. He's in a precarious situation." Then she turned to Kash and smiled her charming smile, the one that said everything was going to be all right, and she squeezed his arm. "I know you're terrified right now, but I promise, all we want to do is help, Kash."

"So you're gonna take responsibility for him?" Sorren grunted, shifting his feet. "Because I want that on the record for the council."

Okay. He was done keeping his flappy lips shut. To hell with Nina and her ultra-scary gaze. "*The councccil?*" he barked in anger, the word sliding from his lips in a slur. "What is...what wrong wif...*with* you people? What kind of twisted shit do you have going on here? I's gettin' the hell outta here and I...*I'm* gettin' out now!" He tried to wave his finger for effect, but it felt like a limp, squiggly worm.

"The drugs are kicking in, girls..." Marty warned.

Nina made a grab for him with a growl, but it was Wanda who yelped with a tone that said she'd had it up to her eyeballs, "Okay, okay, okay! Enough is enough. It's time we show him, ladies!"

And then...

Well...then stuff happened. Stuff he couldn't unsee. Stuff he couldn't explain—couldn't even begin to explain.

As a for instance, when he'd decided to make a run for it despite Nina's growling protests and Marty's leveled warning, Marty tackled him before he'd made it two feet.

When he was able to gather his wits enough to see

what he saw...the stuff he couldn't unsee...he fought a total blackout.

Of course, the drool dripping from Marty's mouth onto his chin—her werewolf mouth—kept him conscious.

Temporarily anyway.

SEVEN

"**A**s his doctor, I'm going to say this one last time." Scotty shook a stern finger under the enormous merman's nose. "No. You may not see my patient. You also can't call him Paranormal Gumbo. It's very offensive. You should know better in this day and age. His name is Kash Samuels. Yes, he's showing signs of several paranormal afflictions, but we haven't been able to parse what's valid and will stick, and what will peter out and be overruled by something else. Understood?"

The large man with a body like Jason Momoa and hair the color of the setting sun thinned his lips. "But—"

"But nothing! This isn't some shelter where all you council members and pack leaders claim your paranormal pet. We don't have all the facts, and while it's awesome you're all taking responsibility for the society members who were involved in the incident, your honesty is noted but, at this point, unwarranted. No one sees Kash Samuels until he's fit to be seen. Please pass that on to the line outside."

With those curt words, Scotty pushed her way through Kash's door, leaving Nina to guard him from the big merman.

There literally was an actual line of people hoping to talk to Kash. Man, the paranormal world had changed so much, due in great part to the women of OOPS.

They'd turned what used to be a disaster of epic proportions, a secret you hid from anyone and everyone, into an almost trendy event.

No longer filled with shame and regret, a paranormal incident was now considered manageable by all but the very old guard, and even some of them had come around. That was all due to Nina, Marty and Wanda.

They preached acceptance and tolerance and, above all, compassion. No one had to die because they'd mistakenly breached the world between human and the paranormal through no fault of their own.

Still, there were some old curmudgeons who'd like to end anyone who invaded their world—mistake or not. Social media played an enormous part in that. It wasn't like the days of yore, when it was hard to get the word out. Nowadays, all it took was one reckless jackass with an inflated ego and a Facebook account.

Should word get out that turning into a vampire or whatever without consequences was possible, every teenager from here to eternity would find a way to become the next *accident*.

That would jeopardize a lot of people, including her parents and her entire clan.

So she'd better figure out how to help this man and hurry up about it.

Scotty stared down at Kash, his beautiful face serene in his drug-induced sleep, and wondered what the hell to do with him.

So far, she'd identified six different strains of paranormal traits. Werewolf, vampire, bear, merman, dragon and demon, with a skosh of angel thrown in for dichotomy kicks.

But none of them had fully fleshed out at this point. No one trait was dominant. Though, he did have a paw the size of a baseball mitt, which was going to leave him thrilled to bits when he woke up and saw how enormous it was—not to mention how long his nails were.

"You, sir, are in dire need of a pedi," she joked, tucking the blanket around his legs, careful to avoid his colorful fin.

"Fuuuck, that's a big ol' paw, huh, Doc?" Nina came to stand next to her.

When Scotty was about to protest her presence, Nina held up a hand. "Don't worry. Wanda's got a handle on that shit out there. No one'll even think about giving her shit. She's got her stern teacher face on."

Scotty chuckled low. "Have I mentioned it's nice to meet you guys? You're everything people said and more."

Nina scowled, and if one could imagine, her exceptionally beautiful face grew even prettier when she did. "I don't know what the fuck that means. Unless it means people talk smack about us all the time because instead of *eliminating* the damn problem like they used to, we fucking love it to death instead."

This time, Scotty's head fell back on her shoulders when she laughed at this woman in a T-shirt that read, "Thou shalt not try me. Mood 24:7"

"I've heard a lot of stuff, and sure, there's been some grumbling about not following the old-world orders, but mostly it's been pretty positive."

The vampire grunted, crossing her long arms over her chest. "Yeah. I'm sure all the shit they say about me is positive. But fuck 'em and fuck their stupid rules. If it wasn't for what those sappy bitches out there did for me, I'd be dead. I don't forget shit like that. Ever. So I do what they ask me to fucking do because they're important to me."

Scotty's heart warmed at that. She didn't have friends who were as close as these women were. There'd been a couple in college, but being her friend meant a wealth of issues that were hard to deal with when you were a young, healthy paranormal with a nightlife to lead, bars to explore, and dorm hopping to be had.

She cocked a suspicious eyebrow upward as she looked at Nina. "Are you saying you'd rather kill the people you guys help instead of helping them integrate?"

"Don't be obtuse. Of course not. I'm an asshole, but I'm not *that* much of an asshole. I'm just saying, I probably wouldn't bake cookies and coddle the fuck out of 'em with bedtime stories and trips to the fucking mall. Those two out there are too damn soft. What some of these shits need is a good kick in the pants to jumpstart their asses. You know, light a fire under 'em."

Scotty grinned up at this fierce woman. "Uh-huh. That's what everyone says you say, but your actions and, apparently, your Zoom account say something else entirely."

Nina flipped her middle finger under Scotty's nose. "Fuck off. I only have a Zoom account because those two made me get one so we can keep in touch with our cases."

Scotty winked and nudged Nina in the ribs. "Right. Otherwise, you'd write them off and never talk to them again once you knew they were safe. Got it," she mocked.

Nina gave her a lopsided grin, but she still scoffed. "Whatever. The point is, I don't know if I'd be as easy-going as they are. End of story. Now where the fuck do we stand with Mr. Paranormal As Fuck?"

Scotty sighed, still unsure what to do with this gorgeous man. "Well, I've managed to identify five strains of paranormal and one that's iffy and will likely make his life a virtual hell."

Nina clucked her tongue. "Demon and angel?"

"Yep."

She laughed but then she sobered. "All we need is Lucifer or one of his minions showing the fuck up. That won't be good."

Scotty shivered and rubbed her arms. "You're right. That terrifies me. There are plenty of paranormal who've come to a place of acceptance, but Lucifer sure isn't one of them. He'd claim Kash and that would be that."

The woman she'd heard so much about, the one who'd die before she'd let harm come to the vulnerable, made an appearance. "The fuck I'd let that happen, or at least I'll go down swingin' tryin' to stop it."

Scotty gripped Kash's wrist to check his still thready pulse. "Right, Marshmallow."

She held up her hands like two white flags, palms facing forward. "Ooo, shots fired."

"Just the facts, ma'am," she said on a laugh, and then she frowned. "Did he seize again when you guys scared him witless with The Greatest Paranormal Show on Earth, or did he just collapse?"

"We didn't do it the fuck on purpose. Someone had to prove to him we're telling the truth so he'll quit flaking on us. It's dangerous for him to freeball all over Buffalo, for Christ's sake. And no seizure. He just passed out. But Marty was drooling all over him with her scary werewolf face. So, there's that."

Scotty didn't say anything, but she hoped the lack of a seizure was because he was stabilizing.

Nina stared down at him, too, and then she asked, "What's up with *you*?"

"Meaning?"

"Don't play fucking coy. You know what I mean. You're a human with two vampires for parents who didn't adopt you and you're in a wheelchair. I wanna know why—on both counts."

Scotty didn't hate her direct nature as some surely would. She'd much rather have Nina's approach. "I'm an anomaly. No one knows how my mother ended up pregnant, let alone gave birth to a human. My folks are old-school vampire. Centuries old. As you well know, vampires don't usually procreate. The wheelchair thing is because I get tired easily. A side effect of the disease I have."

She shoved her hands into the pockets of her jeans, her glossy hair falling over her shoulder when she leaned into Scotty. "And that disease is...?"

"Kabalo syndrome. It affects my immune system, which leaves me weak sometimes and smaller than average. It also screws with my connective tissue and my heart. My heart is too small to keep up."

Scotty didn't hate speaking the words out loud. She might not have learned to totally compartmentalize her emotions, but when it came to her disease, she had things in hand.

She had one mission and one mission alone, find a way to cure herself. She focused on that rather than her limitations.

"That's a laundry list of shit wrong. I s'pose that means you're pretty sick."

She winced comically. "Well, it ain't good, Marshmallow."

"Be fucking straight with me," Nina demanded, her eyes intense.

"Yes. I'm pretty sick. Not at this particular moment, but something always crops up. It's been that way all my life. I catch every bug known to man, my muscles are weak, and my heart is forever giving me fits and starts with my breathing. I've been on more medication than a pharmacy has shelves to hold them. Nothing's really worked for long and eventually, I'll run out of medications to try."

They stood silently for a moment, and then Nina turned to her, her eyes searching Scotty's with the kind of empathy she claimed she lacked. "So I'm going to ask a stupid fucking question and you can tell me to piss off if it offends you."

"I live for stupid questions."

"Why haven't you had someone turn you? You have to have paranormal friends, right? I know it's against all the fucking rules upon rules they have, but nobody has to know, do they? If you just had an accident?"

Now she scoffed, tucking her hair behind her ears. "Oh, believe me, I've tried. Know what?"

"What?"

"It didn't work. Not only am I an anomaly, I'm an un-turnable anomaly."

"No shit..." Nina whispered.

"No shit. I've been bitten, scratched, you name it. Nothing. Well, except the scars to prove it." She lifted her hair from the side of her neck and pointed to the scar her vampire friend Eden had given her when she'd tried to turn her one very drunk night.

Nina's eyes widened. "Okay, that's pretty fucked up."

"Try explaining why you almost bled out to your very serious, very stern vampire father. *That's* fucked up."

She made a face before she appeared to sympathize. "So, what happens. Do you just keep deteriorating?

"Yep." And soon. "Unless I find a cure."

"And if you don't?"

"I die."

EIGHT

"Janet?" A tongue like a wet flapjack clapped him across the face.

Kash groggily came to the surface of the black hole he'd been floating in and felt another slap of his dog's tongue on his cheek before the weight of the bed sagged and she sprawled across his chest.

He smiled and without even opening his eyes, massaged her neck. This was definitely his Janet. He'd know her if he were deaf and blind just by the feel of her massive fur-covered neck.

Considering drifting back off, something he did a lot of now that he was retired, he was relieved to discover he'd only had a nightmare.

"Remind me never to loan Uncle Garrick the car again, would ya?" Kash whispered into the room. "Phew, I had some crazy dreams, kiddo."

She tucked her solid head into his chest, making him hunker down deeper into the bed.

Every time he thought about her not being on this Earth because the shelter needed space for incoming dogs, his heart shuddered in his chest.

He realized that was the way the world worked. Kash had done plenty of volunteer work for shelters and adoption drives. He was fully aware of the realities of shelter life for a dog, and he hated that Janet, or any animal, spent even a second in discomfort.

She'd come at a time in his life when the world felt as though it was finally coming together for him. As a foster kid, he'd always wanted a dog. There'd been many in his life, but they'd always been someone else's, and when he was shuttled off to a new foster family, he had to leave them behind. That had almost always been harder than leaving his actual foster parents.

He loved animals, and when Janet had come across his timeline as he was scrolling Facebook one day, he was at a place in his life where he was close to handing most of the business over to Garrick and taking some time to get his personal life in order. So he'd deemed it the right time to finally have an animal to love.

Kash also wanted a wife and children, and he was looking for someone who wanted the same. The beginning of that journey for him was a pet of his own. One that needed a soft place to land. One that no one else wanted.

He knew what it was to be unwanted—he'd felt that way all his life. His hope was to give a good life to a dog or a cat and fill the hole of emptiness that being cast aside left behind. His intention was to fill his home with pets, but for the moment, one had been the goal.

That's when he saw Janet. A two-year-old stray, taken in after someone had found her eating rocks behind an IHOP. She had a broken leg, a heart murmur, plenty of scars, and a healthy fear of humans.

From the moment Kash saw her big brown eyes, anxious and afraid, her black and white ears standing upright, her body tense and vulnerable, huddled in a corner, she had spoken to him.

And he'd answered, rushing to the shelter to adopt her. He'd never forget almost missing the deadline and begging the shelter's receptionist to let him in because it was only two minutes after closing.

He'd eventually convinced the manager of the place to let him have Janet after the promise of food donations for life and an adoption day at the restaurant.

Kash had taken her home and they'd never looked back. With patience and a lot of love, they'd bonded. She was the peanut butter to his jelly and it had been that way for three years now.

He hugged her close, considering going back to sleep, but he knew she'd want to eat soon. There wasn't a meal Janet didn't like and with good reason—she only ate the best of the best.

Scratching her neck, he asked, "You hungry, little lady?"

Janet moaned...but then he heard someone coo, "She ate. Isn't that right, sugarpuff? Auntie Nina hooked you up with Uncle Arch and he made you a feast fit for the queen you are, didn't he, beautiful girl?"

No. No. *Noooo.*

Last night hadn't been a nightmare in the traditional sense after all. It had been one in the living sense. Well, shit. What a letdown.

There was a nudge to his arm, hard and confident. "You want me to give her second breakfast?"

He scrunched his eyes tighter and swallowed.

"Oh, open your eyes, Kash Samuels, and stop being such a pissy pants." The wholesome warmth of Wanda's voice penetrated the cozy haze he'd been enjoying. "Janet's here and everything's going to be all right."

"How...*how* did Janet get here?" He'd left her in doggie daycare with a cute kid named Nissa, three days ago at the facility where he always left her if he had to travel.

"Nissa. She's awesome. Five stars, definitely fucking recommend," Nina chirped.

But it might be time to talk to Nissa about giving his dog to strangers.

"Aw, don't be a dickknuckle. Nissa did the right thing, but she only did it because I glamoured her, or whatever the fuck kids call it these days."

Kash popped open one eye and saw Nina, as gorgeous as ever, standing by the side of his bed, making him hug Janet closer. "*Glamoured?*"

She reached out and stroked Janet's head, smiling at her when she nuzzled against Nina's hand. "Read her mind, put suggestive thoughts in her fucking head, whatever. It's a vampire thing we're not supposed to do, but it was an emergency. These two saps said your fucking dog would make you feel better, and there's nothing I live for more than to make Kash Samuel's life, an accidental fucking nightmare, better."

"Nina," Marty warned. "Don't be a dick about it. You agreed it would help, too. Plus, you know you secretly wanted to meet her because you love all animals and it upset you that Janet might have to be in doggie daycare longer than was necessary. In fact, it was Nina who sat in the back with her in the car all the way back here."

The idea that they'd brought Janet to him both comforted and scared the shit out of him. The comforting part was obvious. The scared part had to do with the idea that they knew private details about him he wasn't sure he wanted them to know.

Looking at Marty, and totally avoiding Nina's piercing gaze, he squeaked out a question. "How did you find out where she was?"

"Someone found your phone at NOPE and pictures of Janet were on it, which led us to the fact that you had a dog. We were worried she might be alone, so we did some digging," Marty explained, cupping Janet's muzzle and stroking it with her thumb. "That's how we found the text messages between you and Nissa, at Janet's daycare. We thought she might help you recover and it wouldn't hurt to get in touch with her because she hadn't heard from you in a couple of days."

But his phone had a passcode. How the hell did they get into it?

Nina dropped kisses on Janet's nose, and his dog —*his* dog—ate it up, closing her eyes and sighing happily. "We do this kind of shit all the time, Kash. I mean, I wouldn't have done it. I'd have gone and gotten Janet and taken her home with me and let your ungrateful ass and your kooky bear paw rot outside in the forest because good girls like her should be sitting by a roaring fire, eating GD steak bites while their masters run around, behaving like dumbasses. But like I said—these two sappy, clappy—"

"It was easier than you think," Wanda interrupted, smoothing her hand down her green silk shirt. "Suffice it to say, we know a lot of people who are tech savvy. We're only trying to help make you as comfortable as possible."

There was the fact that he had a paw. His eyes strayed to it briefly before quickly looking away.

Guilt stabbed his gut. Okay. Okay. It wasn't their fault he'd stopped at a bar and gotten his ass kicked, and maybe they really were trying to "help" him. But he was still struggling with the cult theory.

Wanda scratched Janet's hindquarters, managing to find her favorite spot. His heart dog rolled her traitorous sixty pounds of love over and showed her belly, a sure sign she trusted them.

And if Janet trusted them...

There'd been a woman he'd dated a few months back. Selma. Selma Sanchez. Beautiful, smart, an attorney and alleged animal lover, just like him.

Janet was always fearful of new people at first. You'd never know it by the way she was cozying up to these women, but she was usually at least a little tentative.

But with Selma? She hid under the bed *always*. Janet's favorite thing to do was snuggle on the couch and watch TV with him, but when Selma came over, she'd stay in another room and nothing, not even her favorite pig's ear treat, could coax her out.

In fact, Kash always knew when she was about to ring his doorbell due to the fact that Janet would excuse herself from the living room and sleep under the bed.

One day, he discovered why. Selma had let herself in when he wasn't home. Apparently, Janet had thrown up on one of her beloved shoes and just as he'd entered his house, he caught Selma in the act of throwing that shoe at Janet's head while she called his dog a name he wouldn't repeat, but it rhymed with stunt.

Of course, there'd been signs he'd brushed off. Sure, Janet shed and got her hair all over everything he owned, and yes, she was gassy, but a true animal lover understood that came with the territory.

Needless to say, Selma was gone in two seconds flat—which turned out to be just as well. His brother had a conversation with one of Selma's ex-friends who'd told him she'd only been dating him for his money and she mostly hated Janet.

So that Janet appeared to love these women, wasn't at all afraid of them, said something.

Pushing himself to a sitting position, Kash acknowledged their act of kindness. "Thank you for bringing her to me. She's the most important thing in my life."

"That's more like it," Nina said, cuddling Janet's head against her chest. "Tell Daddy you catch more flies not being a fucking dick."

Scotty poked her head between the women standing around the bed and slipped between them. Man, despite his circumstance, he couldn't help but think about how pretty she was. Petite, and not usually the type of woman he gravitated toward.

Still, he found himself drawn to her. When she smiled at him, she stirred up a cache of weird emotions he'd have to chalk up to the immediacy of his desperation and possibly a little bit of savior complex.

Brushing her hands together, Scotty said, "Now that we've determined your level of dickery, let's make a deal, Kash Samuels."

He watched as she, too, stroked Janet's back, and fought a smile. "A deal?"

She bobbed her dark head, her thick chestnut hair falling around her face from the motion. "Yep. A deal. Look, you can't go around looking like this. Even you have to admit there's a problem. You do see your tail and your fin, don't you? And lest ye forget about your paw..." Scotty grabbed his hand and held it up with a warm chuckle.

His lips thinned in disgust. "I do. I don't want to, but I do."

Janet licked Scotty's hand and her eyes lit up as she acknowledged his answer. "Okay, so if you keep running away, how do you plan to live like this? Are you prepared for the questions your neighbors alone will have?"

Oooo. Yeah. That was fair. Joanie Mason, soccer mom, neighborhood know-it-all and busybody, would definitely have something to say about the shape he was in.

"That's fair," he conceded as she looked at him, her beautiful eyes so round and serious he could get lost in them.

"Then let's do this. Marty has graciously offered

her guesthouse to you and Janet—to us, actually. It's but a walk away. We can stay there while we figure this out. This way, you can have the comfort of a home setting and Janet can be with you instead of missing you in doggie daycare, and maybe I can figure out how to regulate what's happening to your body."

"Marty's guesthouse is beautiful, Kash, and there's plenty of space," Wanda assured him with a smile. "Two bedrooms, two bathrooms, a newly renovated kitchen and plenty of space for Janet to roam in a fenced-in backyard."

Marty agreed with a nod of her blonde head. "Yep. It's almost nicer than my house. And she can hang out with our dogs, Waffles and Muffin. Muffin's older, but Nina's dog Waffles is gonna love playtime with Janet."

Nina had a dog? Like, *what*? "You have a dog? Don't vampires eat dogs?"

Nina rolled her dark eyes, jamming her hands into her jeans. "No. We eat jackoffs like you. I'd just as soon hurt a dog as I would a fucking kid, weirdo, but if you keep it up with all this shock and awe about my softer side, I'll pop your eyeballs out and eat 'em like malted milk balls. Now shut the fuck up and let the doc help you get your sorry lot in life together."

"What Nina means to say is, yes, she has a dog named Waffles, who is paralyzed and has a wheel-chair. Marty has a dog, too. Her name is Muffin, and both dogs live better lives than we could ever hope for simply being the cherished pets of these women,"

Scotty said. "Now, back to what I was saying. You can't wander around like this. Not only for your safety, but the safety of others."

He lifted his chin. "Meaning?"

Scotty popped her lips, straightening her white lab coat. "Meaning, let's say as a for instance you're a werewolf, which your tail and body hair growth would certainly support. There are plenty of precautions that have to be taken—it isn't just about the shift and the change in your body, Kash. There are urges...urges you don't know how to control until you're taught. Urges that can hurt people."

The memory of Marty atop him, snarling and drooling was enough to unsettle him. He hugged Janet tighter. "Urges..." He repeated the word as though he didn't understand what it meant, but only because it was utterly astounding to him.

"Yes, urges," Marty reiterated. "And I *can* help you with those. We can help you with most of your new traits in one way or another, but there's more to this than just changes in your body and the urge to behave like a werewolf."

"Like the fact that at any given time, a motherfucker from the pack council or a vampire clan or any leader of a paranormal group could just wipe your ass out because you're a goddamn inconvenience. Not everyone feels the way we do, buddy. Not everyone wants you to skip on outta here and live a happy paranormal eternity. Some of the older guard would just as happily kill you because they don't want to teach you how to be paranormal. You're not only a potential danger to yourself, but a danger to others, too. Now, if you don't care about that shit—run the fuck away. I'll take Janet and go the hell home."

And Janet would probably go with her, judging by the dreamy-eyed gaze she cast upon Nina.

Wanda sighed and rubbed her temples. "What Nina *should've* said is, our biggest goal is to keep you safe while we teach you how to live this new life that's been so callously thrust upon you, and prevent you from hurting someone else in the process. The danger from our world is very real."

"If you'd like, I could let you take a peek at the line that runs all the way down the hall, filled with the paranormals who want to take responsibility for you. I'm pretty sure not all of them are as friendly as these ladies," Scotty said with a wince, hitching her thumb over her shoulder.

Kash gulped, forcing his voice to work. "So you're telling me, someone might want to kill me for a mistake I didn't even damn well make?"

What kind of bullshit was that?

Wanda's voice was quiet when she responded. "That is a distinct possibility."

"So I guess outpatient care is out of the question?" he half-joked, looking to Scotty.

"Well, seeing as you live an hour away, and I can't exactly pack all this in my handy-dandy medical bag,"

Scotty spread her arms wide to encompass the room full of medical gadgets, "I'd have to give it a thumbs down. But I swear to you, I only want to help, Kash. I won't do anything without your consent, and I'll explain it all in as much layman detail as I can. You just have to give me the chance and at least try to trust me."

Trust. That was a tricky word for Kash—for both Samuels brothers, but especially for him.

Yet, it appeared he could either risk being killed by one of these nuts or be Scotty's test dummy. Were those the two choices?

Oh c'mon, Kash, that's not fair. First, you have a bear paw. Explain that to the masses, would ya? Scotty's not doing this so she can use you as a lab rat. I think deep down you know that. She's trying to help—and if you think Janet likes the other women, look at the way she stares at the pretty doctor.

His eyes scanned Janet's expression of pure bliss as Scotty scratched her ears—and he made a leap of faith.

"And what do you get out of this?"

"You want honesty?" she asked, staring straight at him.

Kash nodded. "That's all I want."

"This is something that's never happened in the paranormal world before. It's groundbreaking. I want to study it, figure it out, see how to regulate it. I want my name on it. Call it a feather in my scientist's cap. Is that honest enough?"

That was pretty honest.

"Then okay."

Scotty's head popped up, her eyes gleaming at him. "*Okay*-okay?"

He sighed, ragged and long, running a hand through his hair. "Okay-okay. Do what you need to do to in order to get my...my whatever together. But I want to be perfectly clear, I'm doing this with enormous reservations and based only on the fact that you have to give me your word I can walk whenever I want. If so, then we have a deal."

Scotty stuck her hand out toward him. "It's a deal."

Kash gave her his paw, and she giggled.

He supposed he should feel like he was making a deal with the devil for all the resistance he'd given them, but when their hands touched, and he engulfed Scotty's very small one in his, he didn't feel like that at all.

Rather, Kash felt a tingle—one that slithered from his fingers along the skin of his arm, and for the moment, he'd attribute that to his condition.

Yep. He was just in a vulnerable position. Nothing to see here.

Nothing.

CHAPTER

NINE

"Wel...come hooome," Carl said, smiling shyly at Scotty and Kash.

"Wow," they both muttered as they entered Marty's "guesthouse."

They stood in the foyer while Scotty's eyes processed the beauty before her. Starting with the dark gray stone beneath her feet, to the puffy camel-colored couch with soft blue and beige puffy pillows and cozy throw blankets.

There was a literal wall of a stone fireplace where a roaring fire gusted, complete with an orthopedic dog bed for Janet on the hearth. A small vintage desk and lamp sat under the crosshatched windows, through which snow fell at a rapid pace.

"Cute, right?" Marty acknowledged as she slipped past them and headed to the kitchen where she dropped eight or ten bags of groceries. "We did a total renovation on it this past summer. It was long past time for an update. I was going for rustic French countryside after a trip my husband and I took a couple of years ago to Provence."

"Aka, Marty needed a reason to fucking drag us to a bunch of home decorating stores," Nina snickered, following her friend into the kitchen with even more grocery bags.

"Well, I'd say mission accomplished. It's beautiful, Marty."

The kitchen...what an absolute dream. Scotty could appreciate a beautiful, functional kitchen, seeing as hers was the size of a shoebox.

She lived simply despite the fact that technically, she was rich—inherited rich, anyway. Who had time for decorating when you were trying to find a cure to keep you alive?

Still, she adored this amazing vibe Marty had created.

From the moss-green cabinets that reached the ceiling to the dusty-charcoal stone countertops and matte black appliances, Scotty had kitchen envy.

"OMG!" she squealed in sheer delight when she looked into the brick alcove built around the stove. "You have a pot filler!"

Marty smiled, her eyes twinkling. "It's the simple things, isn't it?"

It damn sure was. She made a lot of big pots of soup to freeze. Living in Syracuse gave her plenty of opportunity to need the warmth. Having so much trouble with her muscles, which were oftentimes weak, making a trip back and forth from her sink to her stove was a chore. A pot-filler would ease some of that burden.

Wanda held out her hand to Scotty with a warm smile, pulling her toward a short but wide hallway with light oak flooring.

"Come with me, choose your bedroom before the Burgermeister gets there first."

Scotty chuckled at the nickname Nina had bestowed upon Kash. She thought it befitting a guy who owned a burger joint. He, on the other hand, didn't appear to enjoy it as much as they did.

As Wanda tugged her along the hallway, the walls tastefully decorated with gorgeous, muted florals and pictures of sheep and cows grazing, they stopped at bedroom number one.

Painted in another shade of soft gray, the bed, a huge king-size with an antiqued white headboard nested in the corner of the wall, drew your eyes immediately.

A light beige coverlet sprawled across its surface, with a blue-and-cinnamon-striped duvet folded at the foot. There had to be at least eight cushy pillows lining it in matching colors, and a gorgeous area rug lie beneath the bed's sturdy legs.

"Oooo, it's almost like a hug," Scotty breathed,

inhaling the beauty of the calm she experienced simply by being in the room.

She wanted to snuggle up in a blanket in the window seat with all the beautiful pillows and read a good book as the snow fell in splotches of white.

"Wait till you see the bathroom," Wanda encouraged, pointing to the middle of the room.

Scotty padded across the floor, loving the feel of the hardwood beneath her feet. She stuck her head inside, her eyes widening.

Timeless black and cream checkerboard marble tile, dull and muted to appear rustic, covered the floor. The vanity, obviously once a dresser, now refinished and stained black with brass pulls, housed a gray stone sink, lightly veined.

And the shower? It took up an entire wall with its gold fixtures and blue glass tiles in a chevron pattern.

Wanda snickered as she nudged her. "Told you."

"And she calls this a guesthouse? Cripes. My whole apartment could fit into the bathroom alone." Scotty ran her fingers along the oyster-colored board and batten on the wall. "It's amazing. I'm so grateful to have such a beautiful place to come back to after a long day at work."

Wanda's smile was warm. "Marty likes to decorate and she's really good at it. Now, want to see the other room before you decide?"

But Scotty shook her head, fighting off a wave of dizziness. "Nope. This is perfection. The shower and that bench in it alone are reason enough not to look any further."

"Then I'll have Darnell bring your bags to you. Do you want to nap before dinner? Arch is cooking. A girl needs her rest before she has a meal by Arch. Believe me. I speak from experience."

Scotty flapped a dismissive hand at Wanda. "Nah. I'll be fine."

But Wanda gripped her arm. "Look, Nina explained your health situation, and I won't pry, and I'll try not to sound like a mother hen, but I don't want you to tax yourself. Your father says you have a tendency toward overworking to the point of exhaustion. That's not why we hired you, Scotty."

Scotty bristled, lifting her chin. "My father? You spoke to him?"

She gave her a crooked grin and winked. "I don't think I had a choice, but of course, as an upper-echelon member of the vampire community, he heard what happened with Kash and called my husband, Heath, who directed him to me. After speaking with him, I get the impression he isn't one to be ignored."

Scotty made a face, her eyes narrowing as she looked out the big window facing the forest. "My father is an overbearing pain in my tush. He's more concerned about me representing his reputation properly than he actually is about me."

She realized she'd come across as a little bitter, but

her parents just wouldn't let her live her life. It was always about keeping up appearances with them.

Or correction, that was the way with her father.

"While that's quite possible, we, on the other hand, don't give a schmutz about our reputations. We just want you to pace yourself, okay? This isn't a sprint —it's a marathon."

If only... if her blood tests kept coming back with such shitty numbers, it was only a matter of time...

Shaking off her anger, Scotty nodded. These women weren't without empathy—not if the way they handled the kind of life-altering events they encountered was any indication.

"I'm sorry, Wanda. My dad is my hang up and sometimes I forget not to take it out on other people."

"No worries. Just understand, no matter what, we're on your side. Kash's, too." She squeezed Scotty's arm for emphasis.

Scotty swallowed hard. "Listen, can we keep my... my health issues between us? I need Kash to have confidence in my abilities. I don't want him thinking about anything other than becoming who he's meant to be. My...*stuff* can become a hinderance. A real downer to a healing patient."

Wanda's expression read concerned. "We'll do whatever you want, but I get the impression Kash is a pretty decent human being. I'm sure he'd want to make everything as easy as possible for you, knowing your condition."

She swallowed hard, her heart skipping a beat. "That's one of many reasons I'd prefer he didn't know."

Wanda held a finger to her glossed lips. "Then mum's the word."

"Thank you. He's already not thrilled about being here. I'm glad you found Janet. It'll make my job a little easier."

Wanda tucked her hand into the pocket of her skirt and sighed. "Well, quite frankly, who'd be thrilled about being ripped from their life and hurled into a boxing ring with fang-showing, anger-management-needing Nina? As if that's not enough, then try adjusting to having a tail, a fin, a bear paw, some pink hair, a piece of a wing, and what looks like a snaggle tooth."

She'd forgotten about his newest affliction. One gnarly, jagged incisor had made an appearance as they'd prepared to bring him to the guesthouse. If you looked at Kash as a whole picture, it was hilarious. In fact, it was hard to keep her laughter in check.

But Wanda was right. This was a rough card he'd been dealt. Add in Nina and it became just a little hellish.

"You're right, and I'll try to keep that in mind. I'm trying very hard to keep things professional. I've been accused of getting too involved a time or two, and I promised myself I wouldn't do that this time. But I struggle to find the balance between empathy and medical stoicism."

"Is it hard because he's cuuute?" Marty cooed from the doorway as she dropped some fluffy fresh towels on the bed.

Scotty's cheeks went hot, but she stayed quiet.

Marty winked and gave her a saucy smile. "Well, he is, and you know it, and there's nothing wrong with saying so. I'll say it for you. Kash Samuels, even with a fin, a jenky tail, pink hair, and a snarly tooth, is a lil' hot. Like, fan-yourself hot. It's okay to like him. You won't be the first doctor to fall in love with her patient."

"Marty's ever the romantic," Wanda teased. "No one's fallen in love just yet, Miss Devourer of Romance Novels."

Yet... That scared her to death. She'd done that once and ended up heartbroken. No matter what, she had to keep her head on her shoulders this time.

Just then, Janet burst into the room, her joy obvious as she nudged Scotty's hand. Scotty sat at the end of the bed, looking to Wanda and Marty. "Is she allowed on the bed?"

Wanda tipped her head back and chuckled. "Are you kidding me? That's not even a question when it comes to us. Marty'd let an octopus on the bed." She paused for a moment, pressing her finger to her cheek in thought. "In fact, I wouldn't be surprised if one hasn't already been right in that exact spot, considering all the accidents we've handled. They become a blur after a while. Anyway, do what you think is best. Dinner's at seven and you won't want to miss it. It's beef bourguignon night."

After Wanda grabbed Marty's hand and they took their leave, Scotty smiled at Janet and encouraged her to jump up next to her by patting the bed.

"There you are, little lady," Kash called to Janet from the door.

He entered the room, the fin sprouting from his ankle flapping hilariously as he walked, his tail, ragged and patchy with hair, dragging behind him. Blowing the pink strands of hair from his face, he reached out and cupped Janet's muzzle with a warm smile that made Scotty's insides virtually glow.

"I wondered where you got to."

But Janet didn't budge. She sat solidly against Scotty, pressing her stout body into her thigh. Scotty couldn't help but grin up at Kash. "I think I made a friend."

He smiled back. "I think so. She almost never leaves my side, but she's really branching out with you guys. It's nice to see her so social." Then he looked around at the room and gave a low whistle. "This *guesthouse* is really something, huh? Did you see my room? I swear, the tub's the size of a swimming pool."

"I didn't, but I bet it's beautiful," she said, her eyes suddenly heavy.

He rocked back on his heels and pushed his pink

hair from his face. "It's damn amazing. I guess if I had to land somewhere, this isn't so bad. Beats the Motel Six."

She laughed even as her body began to wind down, sinking deeper into the end of the bed. It'd been a long morning straight into late afternoon. She was pretty wiped out. "It beats my crappy apartment a hundred-fold."

He cocked his head and shot her a teasing smile. "Aren't you a rich doctor?"

She snorted, pulling one of the blankets at the end of the bed over her chilly legs. "Hah! Research scientists don't make a lot of money. I live in a tiny studio apartment with my cat Esperanza—Espy, for short. Named after my beloved nanny when I was growing up. I hope she'll be here shortly. Darnell said he'd send someone to my apartment to grab her for me."

Now he smiled that devastatingly handsome smile —one that said they shared a connection in their love of animals and it made her belly go a little topsy-turvy. "So you're an animal lover, too?"

"I am. Now let's hope our two get along with each other. Espy's never been around dogs."

"Janet's never been around cats. So we'll see how this goes, huh?"

Scotty found herself momentarily lost in his eyes before she shook her head from this daze she was in. "Yeah...I guess so," she whispered.

He motioned to the top of the bed. "Scoot up and get comfortable. You look tired, Dr. Scotty."

She shook her head with a stubborn lurch. "I really shouldn't. I want to run your bloodwork again, maybe give you a cat scan..." And stuff. She just couldn't remember what stuff at the moment.

But Kash insisted, taking her fingers in his and nudging her toward all those delightful pillows. "I promise I'll wake you in a half hour. How's that?"

As she let her head fall to the pillows, and Janet curled up next to her, she gave in. Wanda was right. She needed to keep from taxing herself if she hoped to get anything accomplished.

"Thirty minutes, forty-five tops," she murmured, slinging an arm over Jane's middle and sighing.

"Forty-five tops," he whispered huskily, dragging a blanket over her, tucking it under her chin and around her legs.

She couldn't remember the last time she'd felt this comfortable.

Or if she'd ever felt this comfortable.

But it was lovely. So lovely.

TEN

" I feel like I could run on this thing forever without ever getting out of breath," Kash commented as she monitored his erratic heartbeat while he jogged on the treadmill.

Without a shirt.

Because he'd been working up a sweat. But it was the dead of winter in Buffalo, and she couldn't very well turn the air on to cool the basement lab the women had constructed for her in Bobby-Sue Cosmetics, not without freezing out everyone else in the building.

There was always the danger she might overheat, though.

Damn it all, Kash Samuels was so pretty. His abs rippled like a pond as his muscled arms swung back and forth and he ran, attached wirelessly to a bunch of machines by electrode pads.

Scotty forced herself to look away and focus on the heart monitor. "That's the paranormal in you. You have super-strength now and super-speed. There could be a chance you'll be able to sense when someone's lying or feel a vibe someone's giving off—discomfort, anxiousness, subterfuge, even deceit. And etcetera. There are lots of adjectives to support that, but you get the drift."

"I can't say I hate the super-speed," he said with a wry grin. " That's super-*cool*. It's the rest of this I don't love."

She snickered. He was definitely a sight. They'd taped his tail up along his spine to keep it from dragging and impeding his movement. His pink hair, getting longer and pinker by the day, mingled with his shorter dark hair was up in a man bun he despised, but cutting the strands of pink hair did little to nothing.

It sprouted back almost within the day, thicker and more luxurious—so luxurious, she was a little jealous.

Though, his bear paw had improved exponentially. The nails on his fingertips were still a little deadly, but his hand once more resembled a hand, if not a bit hairy.

"Have I mentioned I can smell everything? Even scents that aren't at all familiar to me? I don't mean Marty's perfume or Arch's bacon pie—boy, that man can cook. I mean stuff I don't get. It happened when

I was first at Wanda's, but it kind of faded to black for a little while. Then last night, it came back full force. I think I was smelling the pine trees from inside the house. Like, while I was in bed. Is that insane?"

She had noticed his nose twitching a lot in the last week or so. "Nope. It's not insane, it's par for the course. Vampires can smell blood. Werewolves are known to smell it, too. But they can also smell their life mates, among other various odors."

He ran faster at that comment, his legs pumping hard. "Life mates? Is that stuff really true? I've seen it on plenty of television shows and in movies. But c'mon. I mean, I don't want to knock the way of the were, but it sounds pretty hokey."

She smiled, looking down at his chart to see what his numbers had been last night before he'd gone to bed, not long after yet another incredible dinner. Wanda had promised Arch's cooking would be amazing. She hadn't lied.

The first night, Arch had made the most succulent beef bourguignon she'd ever had, atop a bed of garlic parmesan risotto with baby carrots and peas, followed by a chocolate lava cake and hazelnut coffee.

And every night after that had been as delectable as the first. Seven nights in, and she wasn't sure she ever wanted to leave. Add in the time they spent around the table after a hearty meal, sharing their days and how much she looked forward to the evenings spent with these people, and she definitely never wanted to leave.

To say she'd landed a gem of a job would be an understatement. To be invited to join all these people she'd grown up hearing about, as they interacted and shared meals, felt like a balm to her soul—and a privilege she wasn't worthy of.

Her work was filled with isolation. Long nights in a cold lab with nothing but her microscopes, Bunsen burners and Hot Pocket dinners made for a lonely existence.

She didn't go out for girls' nights or take vacations. She worked. To identify strains of viruses that could kill off paranormals, diseases that affected them differently than they did humans and, mostly, to find a way to cure herself.

But she never took a break. That first night, after Nina had sat on the bed and gently nudged her awake for dinner, the loneliness she usually successful staved off hit her right between the eyes, and as everyone joked and laughed and included her, she felt the beginnings of a bond—the bond every one of their clients enjoyed.

"Scotty? Life mates? Do they really exist? Is it like on TV?"

Kash interrupted her thoughts with his question. She kept her eyes on his chart, pretending to scribble and not look at his chest, damp with perspiration.

"They say it does. If you ask the ladies, they'll tell

you it does. But I think that's a feeling only someone who's experienced it can confirm."

He cocked a raven eyebrow upward in inquiry, his chiseled jaw tight as he ran harder. "So no life mate for you?"

Why, when he looked at her that way, did she want to twirl her hair around her finger and smile shyly? Ugh.

"I'm not paranormal. You know that, right?"

"I think I remember hearing that. And I can't believe I'm saying it as though we're talking about the price of gas." He shot her a wry smile as the treadmill whirred under his feet. "But does that mean you can't have a life mate? Or as the ordinary humans call it, a soul mate?"

"Is that your way of asking me if I'm in a relationship?" The moment the words shot from her lips, she wanted to bite her tongue.

That was a personal question. Shut it down, McNealy.

"I guess it is," he answered and waited for her response.

"If I was in a relationship, would I have moved into the guesthouse for who knows how long? No. No relationship. It's just me and my cat."

Who thankfully *really* loved Janet. After sniffing each other out, they'd ended up first sitting on the hearth together as far apart as they could, before realizing they were meant to cuddle in the big dog bed for Janet.

They'd found her orange and black tabby curled against Janet's midsection, sound asleep, every night since.

When Kash didn't say anything else, she figured the discussion was over. But then he asked, "Aren't you going to ask me if I'm in one?"

"In one what?" She pretended not to know what he meant—even if she really was dying to know. Which was unhealthy, but that didn't mean it didn't exist.

Her eyes caught his smirk. "A relationship."

"Nope." Turning her back to him, Scotty studied the white wall where she'd hung his chart so he wouldn't see her face.

"Well, FYI, I'm not. It's just me and my forever girl, Janet."

Well, yippee for you and Janet.

Fighting a sigh, she bit the inside of her cheek to keep from being spiteful. *Just because you can't have him doesn't mean you should be jealous of his dog because she can. That's just ridiculous and petty.*

"That's nice," she murmured. He was single and so was she. Big dealio.

"Hey, am I really going seventy?"

Scotty looked at the monitor on the front of the treadmill. It was old and it didn't have all the fancy gadgets the fancier models did, but it worked for now until they could get a newer one. "Seventy, yep," she muttered.

Kash's luscious mouth fell open. "You're kidding me? I thought it had to be wrong."

She looked up at him to find a goofy smile on his face as sweat dripped down his cheeks and onto his broad chest, which had just enough hair to be interesting. "I don't kid. So listen, now that we've determined you can run as fast as most paranormals, how about a cool down in the tank? Let's see how long you can hold your breath. Maybe we can inspire the merman in you to come out and play."

He grinned again—the grin that made the deep grooves on either side of his cheeks deepen—as he slowed to a trot. "Okey-doke. So tell me the goal again?"

Walking toward the massive water tank Darnell and Carl had set up and filled for her, Scotty fought a sigh. To be very honest, she didn't really know. In the instance of water people, something she knew little about, Scotty was grasping at straws.

To make it even more difficult, there was almost no one in the paranormal research area who could help with anything but the basics. One of her colleagues literally emailed her and told her to dunk him in a tank and see how long he could hold his breath. He said it might inspire that part of Kash to shine.

Which mostly made sense. *Mostly*.

"The goal is to put you through a bunch of tests specifically designed for each class of paranormal you've been exhibiting, to see if we can encourage your traits to either strengthen or disappear altogether. It's sort of forcing your abilities to perform in a safe, monitored environment. Your seizures worry me, Kash. They tax you to the point of blacking out. I want to figure out how to stop them *before* you pass out—or ideally, stop them altogether so your shifts become smooth."

He grabbed a towel and rubbed it over his face to wipe away the sweat glistening on his forehead. "But I haven't had one since I got here. That's gotta be a good sign, right?"

Scotty shrugged and licked her lips nervously. She simply didn't know and she was honest enough to say as much.

"Maybe, kash. I don't know. It's only been a week. I *do* know I don't want to take any chances. I want a solid month of no seizures before I call it."

She followed behind him toward the tank that looked like it was made for a magic trick for Houdini, keeping her eyes on his shoulder blades, which were also as delicious as the rest of him (even with a half-assed wing), but far less a temptation than, say, his backside, or his long legs poking out of the basketball shorts Darnell had been kind enough to purchase.

The partial wing poking out of his back where his skin puckered had developed some scales, and though sparse, in her professional opinion, they leaned toward dragon.

Kash climbed up the ladder, looked down at the

water, and jumped into the see-through tank before she could give him any kind of instruction. He didn't even appear to think twice.

He hadn't fought her on a single test today, and for that she was grateful, since her limbs felt like mush this afternoon and her breathing was acting up.

Scotty looked toward the tank to offer instructions but...

Oh my word.

If a dry Kash was hot, a wet one was sublime. Scotty swallowed hard as he used his powerful arms to swim to the top of the crystal-blue water. His pink strands of hair had fallen out of the man bun, splaying around his shoulders.

"Lord, that man is a sight, isn't he?" Trina said on a breathy sigh as she entered the lab to stand next to Scotty. "Mm-mm, he's a snack. A whole snack."

No. No. No. No banter about the hot patient today. Eyes on the prize, Scotty. "Trina, could you grab my stopwatch? I want to see how long he can stay under the water before needing to breathe."

"Sure," she said agreeably as she moved closer to Scotty. "But first, can we have a moment of silence for that body—because, honey." Her multicolored wings fluttered and her eyes twinkled.

Trina hadn't been around for Scotty's disastrous relationship with Glen, so she really meant no harm. Not that being sensitive to the fact Scotty had once had an entanglement with a patient that ended with her in ruins was something she expected of Trina.

Regardless, it was highly unprofessional of her to comment on a patient's body.

"The stopwatch, please," Scotty said woodenly, swallowing a snarky remark.

Trina made a face and stomped over to the small desk the ladies had set up for her computer. "All work and no play makes for a dull Scotty."

"Then you'll never be dull, will you?"

Trina cocked her head and narrowed her made-up eyes. "Are you accusing me of not working?"

"Am I?" Scotty lifted her chin as Kash jettisoned upward in the water, using his legs to push him off the bottom of the tank.

She didn't dislike Trina. She acknowledged it irritated her how easy everything was for her—and of course, that she was paranormal. Scotty didn't necessarily want to be a fairy, though Trina's wings were pretty awesome. She'd simply like to be like everyone else in her community—something she'd never take for granted the way Trina did.

Trina squandered her gifts. She relied upon them to obtain the things she wanted rather than earning them. She didn't use her fairy-ness for good. She wasn't out in the paranormal community doing things for others, she was in bars and drinking until she couldn't see straight.

She'd manipulated more than a man or two since

she'd been in Scotty's employ, and it made her incredibly uncomfortable. But her father owed Trina's father, so they were stuck with each other—for now.

Trina pointed a pink nail at Scotty as she flitted across the room to grab the stopwatch, her wings making a blur of colorful motion. "I think you're def poking me, but that's okay. I don't need you to help me enjoy the spoils of a delicious man."

Clenching her fists, Scotty fought not to scream. "Trina—he's a patient. You're in a lab, not some club where you ogle men till you're cross-eyed."

She shrugged her slender shoulders as if whatever Scotty said didn't matter. Not that it ever did. Trina rarely followed any instruction, let alone Scotty's. "You say lab, I say the place doesn't matter. When a man's hot, he's hot."

During their exchange, Kash had busied himself diving up and down, the fin on his ankle flapping furiously. When he popped his head out of the water, clinging to the sides of the glass tank, he called out, "Hey, Boss? Tell me what you need me to do. I'm getting a little soggy in here."

Her eyes met his, but she kept her expression even, though her heartbeat was anything but. "Dive down and stay down until I say to come up for air, or until you can't stay down any longer. I'm going to time you."

Kash gave her a thumbs up and dropped to the bottom of the tank.

"Phew. He can dive down on me any damn day of the week," the fairy murmured, licking her pouty lips.

"Trina! Be professional, *please*."

Scotty wasn't sure what her father owed Trina's, but she was going to have to talk with him, because this was ridiculous.

Trina huffed, her exhalation of breath filled with irritation. "What's next?"

"We monitor him."

"Oooh, I can monitor—"

"His heartrate, his BP, his pulse ox. *Not* his abs," Scotty said with a firm tone.

The moment she finished speaking, something happened. The room grew tense, if that was possible. It became suffocating—the air thick.

Already having problems with her breathing today, Scotty instantly reached for her pocket to dig out her inhaler.

Just as she placed it in her mouth to take a deep breath, the monitor for Kash's heart rate went wild. Unhealthy wild. Her eyes flew to the tank, where he still sat at the bottom, and she motioned him to head toward the surface.

But it was as if he was rooted at the bottom of the tank, his gaze fixated on something... He'd simply stopped moving, his muscles bulging, his feet firmly planted in a defensive stance.

"What the...?" Scotty whirled around to see what he was looking at, but couldn't pinpoint anything unusual. Still, his heart rate continued to climb, the machines beeping wildly, while he either ignored or refused to respond to her signal and surface.

"We have to get him out of the water!" she yelled over the beeping monitors. "He's going to go into cardiac arrest, Trina! Get help!"

Scotty peeled off her lab coat, hoping her jeans and sweater wouldn't weigh her down as she ran toward the tank and began climbing the ladder, fighting to breathe, her heart slamming against her ribs.

When she reached the top, she saw only a quick glimpse of Kash before everything went kerflooey.

He looked like he wanted to take someone out. His expression positively murderous, hard, his eyes like laser beams of rage.

That was when he charged at the tank's wall, like some sort of reckless, mistreated whale at Sea World.

She only briefly thought about how incredible that feat was, considering the amount of pressure he'd have to use to break a glass wall underwater, filled with gallons of liquid.

Scotty stopped thinking when the glass cracked and a beach worth of water, along with Kash, exploded into the lab, crashing and sloshing its way toward the door.

Kash headed straight for Trina with the speed of an F-14 and grabbed her by the neck, holding her small body up like some kind of carnival prize.

Her beautiful wings fluttered, her hands grabbed helplessly at Kash's, but she couldn't get loose.

All the while, Kash was snarling and baring his teeth, but not shifting into anything at all.

And she'd find that odd if not for the fact that this whole thing had just gone Defcon, and now wasn't the time to think about the scientific ramifications.

Not when the last bit of the tank where she was positioned on the ladder began to crumble and you were about to crash to the ground and die a watery death in your own damn lab.

The nerve.

CHAPTER

ELEVEN

"Kash, nooo!" she screamed above the roaring rush of the water as it unfurled its mighty rage.

Where was *roaring* water coming from? The water in the tank should have splashed out, certainly, but roar, with waves? Had Kash done that? What the hell was happening?

But there was no time to give it any more thought. Kash had his hands around Trina's neck so tight, her face went almost purple. She didn't like Trina, but she didn't want her to die.

Then she was falling, the ladder tipping over and dumping her to the floor and she forgot everything but the floor rushing at her.

She hit with a splash, nicking herself on something along the way.

"What the fuck is going on?" she heard Nina holler

as she burst through the door, another impressive feat, considering the amount of water in the lab.

Scotty coughed and sputtered water, stumbling to try to find her feet as water dripped into her eyes. Suddenly, Darnell was there, hauling her upward into his arms as she caught a glimpse of Nina prying Kash's hands from Trina's throat.

"Kash!" Scotty croaked, water spraying everywhere. "Stop!"

"Let her go, motherfucker, or I'm gonna beat your ass!" The vampire grabbed him by the scruff of his wet neck and yanked hard.

Whereas before Kash had been in some weird trance, the order Nina barked snapped him out of his haze. His eyes cleared and instantly he looked around the room, knee-deep in water, as if he didn't know where he was.

Kash's hands went slack and his body loose, his wet shorts clinging to his legs. His chest heaved and his eyes bulged.

He instantly set a terrified Trina down on the floor with obvious care and held his hands up, backing away. "Oh my God. I'm sorry... I don't know... I don't know?"

Nina let the nape of his neck go before spinning Kash around to confront him. "What the fuck just happened there, buddy?" she spat, her hair plastered to her skull in ribbons of ebony resembling wet silk.

But he ignored her question and reached out to

Trina with his good hand, his expression horrified. "Trina, I'm sorry. Shit. I don't know what happened. I'm sorry. I would never hurt someone. I would never hurt you."

Trina backed away, her eyes wide, her makeup streaming down her face, but she quickly followed up with a flippant smile, rubbing her neck with her fingers until she made the red marks from Kash's fingers magically disappear. "I mean, wow, Cowboy. I like it rough sometimes, but for future reference, not *that* rough."

Scotty coughed, her chest and throat stinging from swallowing the chlorinated water. Darnell gave her a sharp pat on the back, making more gurgle up from her throat. She spit it out, using the back of her hand to wipe her mouth.

Darnell, his strong arms gentle, looked down at her with his kind eyes and wiped the wet hair from her face. "You okay, Doc?"

She patted him on the shoulder, took a deep but shuddering breath, and smiled. "I'm okay. You can put me down now, please."

As she dropped to the floor, the water swirling around her calves, she made her way to Kash. Putting a hand on his wet shoulder, and regretting it because it was so strong and warm, she said, "Talk to me. Tell me what happened. What flipped your switch?"

He looked around again, and his gaze screamed confusion. Kash kept scanning the mess of overturned desk and the beakers floating about with glazed eyes. He spread his arms wide. "*I* did this?" he asked in disbelief.

Nina plodded toward them, her eyes flashing. "You sure the fuck did, Burgermeister. So what the shit, man? You wrecked the fucking joint. Not to mention, you made waves. Like, real fucking waves, dude."

Planting his hands on his lean hips, he shook his head, his eyes meeting Scotty's. "I'm sorry. I'll clean it up. I'll pay for the damage—"

"Not necessary," Marty called out from the doorway, where the lessening levels of water now only sloshed around her ankles. "I'll get someone in here to clean this up. But like Nina said, what the eff happened? Are you okay?"

"I..." Kash ran a hand through his tangled wet hair, jerking his fingers out of the strands when they got caught up in the pink lengths.

But Scotty held up her hands to put everyone on pause. "Okay, so you don't remember what happened? What's the last thing you do remember?"

He scraped a hand over the stubble on his chin. "You were talking to Trina about me."

Shit. Shit. Shit. She forgot about his super-hearing. Her cheeks went hot and surely the color of a crisp gala apple.

Hoping to avoid questions, she was about to skirt that subject, but being the good investigators they were, both Nina and Marty asked, "What were they saying?"

Scotty gulped and shivered. Crap.

But Kash shrugged his shoulders with a nonchalant gesture. "Mostly they talked about my stats."

Trina snickered, but Scotty breathed a sigh of relief. "So nothing we were saying triggered you?" she asked.

He squeezed his temples. "I don't think so. I was fine, swimming along, listening to your conversation, marveling at the fact that it was crystal clear."

Perfect. So awesome that he now knew Trina thought he was a god.

"So what the fuck set your ass off, dude? You broke a fucking tank with ten feet of water in it."

"Guess that makes me almost as strong as you, huh?" he joked.

But clearly, Nina wasn't in the mood. Her lips went thin as water dripped down her face and her sodden hoodie. "You got jokes today? How about I hold you under the water until you see your life flash before your fucking eyes?"

He let his head hang in apology, water sliding off his shiny pink hair. "Sorry. I don't remember breaking the glass or going after Trina. I remember hearing Scotty and Trina talk about me— Wait! I do remember *smelling* something."

Marty sloshed farther into the room with a frown

on her pretty face. "Smelled something? *Underwater?* Can mermen smell underwater?"

Kash's expression said he thought it strange, too. "Yeah. It wasn't a familiar smell, either, like perfume or bread baking, you know? Something common that you can instantly pinpoint. I just remember smelling *something*...and then it all goes black."

Scotty frowned, too. "Was it a good smell? A bad smell?"

Kash scratched his chin with the sharp claws of his ever-changing bear paw. "It was unusual. That's all I can say. I don't know how else to define it."

Marty crossed her arms over her chest. "Any particular reason you went for Trina? Or do you think she was just the first thing you saw?"

But Kash shook his head and gave a ragged sigh. "I can't think of a single one."

Nina shoved her hands in her wet hoodie pocket and made a face. "I can't believe I'm gonna fucking ask you this, but I'm gonna fucking ask you. How did you *feel* when you were attacking the poor kid like some kind of fucking wild animal?"

Kash blinked as though a light bulb had just gone off above his head. "Angry. I felt angry, but it was a weird kind of anger."

Scotty blinked, too, as she accepted a towel from Darnell and began drying her hair. "Anger? With Trina?"

"I don't...know. I have zero reason to be angry with her. None. I can't say it makes any sense, but I remember feeling enraged. It's a feeling I know all too well."

"Meaning?" Scotty's heart clenched and she didn't know why. He had gone through something in the past, that much she was sure of—something that had hurt him and left him scarred. But she didn't understand why it plucked at her emotions. They all had baggage.

Kash's jaw went tight and his face hardened, but he didn't give any explanation other than, "Doesn't everyone get angry?"

Darnell clucked his tongue and clapped Kash on the back. "But why Trina, bro? Why would you be angry with her?"

His face relaxed and he shook his head. "Maybe, like Marty mentioned, I just went for the first thing I could get my hands on? I don't know. The next thing I remember is Nina making me let her go."

"Anger is common during the change," Marty pointed out. "I can remember plenty of things triggering me. Little things, big things—all the things."

"Yeah, but you didn't try to kill the lady at the fucking perfume counter because they didn't have any more of that smelly shit you take a damn bath in," Nina remarked.

Marty chuckled. "But I wanted to. That's my point. Surely you remember the shift, Nina. When you went from fully human to half vamp? It's not something you forget."

Nina had a faraway look on her gorgeous face. "It's been so damn long. Almost fifteen years now. Sometimes it feels like I've been a vampire forever, but I was pissed long before I became a vamp. I'm not your girl, if you're looking to base a case on anger alone."

Marty pinched her friend's cheek with affection. "While that's a fair assessment of you Dark Lord, anger, hatred, love, joy, all of those emotions are magnified when you go through the change. What I don't understand, Kash, is why you didn't shift into anything? It's almost feels like you're stuck."

At that precise moment, Kash's tail came undone from his back and fell to the floor with a wet smack, splashing water on them.

There was a brief moment where everyone froze, the air suspended as though holding its breath, until Nina began to laugh. She laughed so hard and so high-pitched, she sounded like a hyena.

And then everyone else laughed with her, including Kash, until tears streamed down their faces and they couldn't breathe.

Well, those who were capable of breathing, anyway.

CHAPTER

TWELVE

K ash entered the bedroom after taking a long, hot shower, a towel wrapped around his waist. His feet padded across the hardwood floor toward the enormous bed, covered in a cream and moss-green duvet with a bazillion pillows he'd crashed hard on last night. Janet sat in the middle of the bed with Espy under her chin.

He plopped down at the end of the mattress and dropped a kiss on the top of her head. "You're ruining Miss Marty's duvet with your hair, little lady. We're gonna have to get a bigger lint brush."

Janet licked his face, making him laugh. Even Espy looked for a cuddle when she opened her eyes and gently pawed his hand. He scratched her ears, Espy purring with contentment, as he tried desperately to remember what had made him behave so appallingly in the lab.

It wasn't just that his life had been upended, that his body was doing all sorts of weird things. Now he'd done something very uncharacteristic of him.

He'd been *violent*.

He'd *wanted* to hurt Trina, but he couldn't decide if it was her he'd wanted to hurt or if anyone in his path would've sufficed. He hardly knew her. Why would he want to harm her?

What he *did* know? Beyond the scent he couldn't identify, he'd also smelled the blood coursing through Trina's veins, right through the glass of that tank, and he'd wanted to taste it—which made him sick to his stomach.

Not just the act itself, but the fact that as much as he hated needles and blood, he'd been willing to attack her anyway.

This was absolute madness.

Yes, he'd been angry in the past. Of course he had. He was a foster kid who'd been dumped in home after home, over and over, and at one time separated from his brother until they'd aged out of the system.

But he'd never been so angry as to provoke an attack. For sure he'd had his share of fistfights, but he'd never started one.

Now he was mauling innocent women for no reason?

He was disgusted with himself, despite what the women said—despite what Scotty said. If he was going to end up a werewolf or a vampire, he didn't want to be a violent one. He'd rather be dead.

The women had all assured him it was normal to have wild mood swings, but they were right to keep a watchful eye on him, because now he wasn't just moody, he was unpredictably violent.

Rising, he went to the closet that Darnell had filled with new clothes and pulled on a sweater and some jeans, blowing his ridiculous pink strands of hair out of the way.

"Kash?" he heard Carl call from behind the door.

According to Scotty, Carl was half zombie, saved by Nina from a witch doctor. He'd rolled with that explanation because really, he didn't know what he considered unbelievable anymore.

But Carl was sweet and gentle, and Janet and Espy loved him. He couldn't deny the kindness of the people whose party he'd crashed.

"C'mon in, Carl."

He tried to put a smile on his face, to hide his distress, but Carl appeared to sense his upset. He put a hand on his arm and patted it with an awkward, jerky gesture. "Are you...oookay?"

Kash smiled back and gave Carl a light grip on his shoulder. He was always afraid he'd break the poor kid if he was too rough. "I am, Carl. Thanks for asking."

His pale green face went soft, his eyes questioning. "Ad...vice?"

Kash's heart clenched. He didn't fully understand

what Carl had gone through, but he sensed that he was grateful and he loved these people beyond measure. And the wonderful thing about that was his people loved him back. To find that kind of love in abundance was rare. He and Garrick had never gotten that lucky.

Kash grinned warmly, his heart full with Carl's genuine interest in his comfort. "If you've got some, I'm all ears, bud."

"Trust. It's okay. Prom...*promise.*" Then he grinned, and Kash's heart tightened to a knot in his chest.

"Knock-knock!" Marty's voice interrupted the moment.

Carl went to the door and popped it open, and Marty stood in the hallway with Nina behind her. The latter held a huge basket covered in green plastic with a big blue bow on top.

"Special delivery, Burgermeister." Nina plodded into the room and dropped the enormous wicker basket on the walnut dresser, giving Carl a quick squeeze on his arm. "I hear Arch is baking in the kitchen, kiddo."

Carl's eyes lit up as he looked at Kash. "Remember wha...what I said. Now, coookies!" He scurried out the door, leaving Kash with the women and a huge basket.

"What is that?"

"It's the pack's way of welcoming you to the fold— or bribing you to find your inner werewolf and come over to the dark side," Marty joked.

"I don't understand."

"It's a basket of fucking meat, dude. Ribeye, filets, fucking like ten porterhouses. It's their way of trying to get you to come to a pack meeting so they can date your ass. Oh, and there's a big box of razors, too."

Kash looked at the mountainous basket and his mouth fell open. He liked a good steak, but...

Marty snorted with a smile. "Werewolves consume copious amounts of meat, and until you can regulate your shifts, you'll need to shave. A. Lot. This is their version of sending flowers. When the council from a branch in Jersey, where one of your assailants is from, found out one of their own had been mixed up in the mess you're in, well, they wanted to make amends."

"A basket of steak is amends for turning me into a werewolf?" Was it him, or was this like offering him an inner tube after crashing into his yacht?

Marty tapped the green plastic on the basket and wrinkled her nose. "The Brazinskis are nothing if not creative. Our pack would have done it differently, of course, but I'm the last accident this pack had, and believe me, no one was sending gift baskets to me."

Nina reached down and scooped up Espy, cuddling her under her chin, the feline's tail winding around the vampire's wrist. "Shit's changed a lot since we were turned, Burgermeister. Be glad they didn't fucking send their most bloodthirsty killer to rip you limb from limb." She paused for a moment and rocked back on her heels. "Man, those were the good old days, huh,

Ass-Sniffer? Now we're woke and sensitive or some shit."

"Oh, Nina, hush," Marty chastised her friend. "We never ripped anyone limb from limb unless they deserved it, and you're as woke as the rest of us. Woke simply means we're aware of others' struggles and we acknowledge them."

"Then we should just call ourselves fucking aware," she complained. "All these damn made-up words and acronyms are ridiculous."

"IKR?" Kash teased.

"Shut up, Paranormal Gumbo, and follow us, we have more shit that came while you were playing Poseidon."

He grabbed the card attached to the basket and opened it. As he read the greeting, he snorted. "They sent their sympathies with an invite to fly to Jersey to meet everyone."

Marty laughed, pointing her finger at him, her bangle bracelets tinkling together. "Told you. Couth isn't their strong suit. Listen, Nina's right. Things have changed. Your reception from the paranormal world has been nothing short of a miracle. And if this isn't proof, there are more goodies waiting for you out in the kitchen. Everyone wants you to join one paranormal group or another, and they've all put on their Sunday Best clothes in an effort to win you over."

Kash tucked the card back into the basket,

confused. "But why? I mean, look at me. I'm an amalgamation of paranormal. Who wants that?"

"They're just fucking covering their asses for now. They know those barbarians did you wrong, and they don't want any shit from the big mucky-mucks."

"Mucky-mucks?"

Marty nodded, a smile on her peachy-pink lips. "The people who rule over each faction of species. You know, like we have a president of the United States and each state has representatives? It's the same with the paranormal. We have people who are, in essence, our president—or whatever you want to call them. They're old, and cranky, and mostly archaic in their thinking."

"And they fucking smell like a damn basement full of dead bodies. But since we came along and dragged everyone out of the closet and forced them to realize the bullshit they'd preached for centuries, was, in fact, bullshit, they've chilled a little." Nina set Espy back on the bed.

Kash leaned on the dresser with his elbow, mostly so he could stay standing. "Bullshit?"

"Yeah. People who are accidentally turned don't have to be automatically dragged to their fucking death for something they had no control over. It was bullshit then and it's bullshit now."

Marty nudged Nina when she grinned at Kash. "See, told ya she was woke. But that said, I want you to keep in mind, there are always going to be monsters hiding under the bed."

He gulped. Were real monsters a thing? Christ. "Monsters?"

He realized he'd only managed to squeak out a single word of response for each bit of information they'd provided, but there were times in all this when he was just beyond complete sentences.

Nina flicked his arm with her fingers. "Fucking people who still believe in the old laws, dude. People who don't want to move the fuck forward. Those assholes still exist, and you're gonna need to learn the difference and watch your ass for the ones who think you're impure."

Impure. He'd been called a lot of things in his time. Bastard, illegitimate, unwanted, but impure was a new one.

Forgetting all the labels thrust upon him, Kash did have a complete sentence he'd been wondering about since he'd begun to accept they meant him no harm. "I'm going to ask a question that probably sounds stupid to you both, but bear with me. I'm trying to learn the way of the paranormal here... Why can't I be a part of *your* pack, Marty—or join Nina's clan?"

Was he really saying those words? He felt like he was asking to join some bizarre high school club. But at least he had a decent idea of what it would be like to be in one of their groups.

He enjoyed their company, quirks and all, and he'd

discovered, he really liked them as people. He liked what they represented. He didn't always love being called fucknuts, but what was in a nickname anyway?

Marty patted him on the arm in what felt like consolation, sympathy written all over her lovely face. "Unfortunately, no. Because we didn't bite you, Kash. It's sort of a territorial thing. But you can always go freelance, too. There are lots of paras who don't have a specific pack or clan. They do their thing. Darnell does that."

Kash scoffed. "I can't say as I blame him there. He's a demon. Nobody wants Satan for a president of their council, do they?"

Marty and Nina both laughed. "Good point. Anyway, it's good to see you coming around about all this. It's life-altering. No one gets that better than us, Kash. All of us. But no matter what you decide, we'll always be here for you, and we'll do our best to teach you how to cope with your new life, with whatever paranormal species you end up being."

He smiled at Marty in gratitude. Somehow, despite all his misgivings, he knew they meant at least that much. "Hey, how's Trina?"

"She's fine, dude. The doc gave her the rest of the day off," Nina assured him.

"And Scotty? How's she feeling? She looked really pale. I'm a little worried she overdid it."

Scotty...

How was he going to keep his attraction to her

hidden? It was all he could do not to ask her all the questions about her personal life.

He'd actually tried for the past week to get her to open up a bit. But she had some kind of wall up, and he didn't understand why. Yet, he wanted to knock it down so he could get to know her.

He found himself endlessly fascinated by her. He loved to watch her concentrate on his medical charts —he loved the line between her eyebrows that popped up when she was deep in thought as she read them.

He loved how she smelled, softly scented with pears and sage. He knew what she showered with because he'd seen the bottle of shower gel when Marty asked him to drop fresh towels for her in her bathroom.

He especially liked when she leaned in to listen to his erratically beating heart with her stethoscope, because then he could get a really healthy hit of her scent.

He loved the way her shiny dark brown hair fell over her shoulders after she pulled out the chopstick thingy she used to hold it up.

She was sexy and smart and elusive as all hell, and when he was in bed at night, Kash wondered if her elusiveness was part of her appeal.

He'd heard Trina talking about his looks today when he was in the tank, but Scotty hadn't said a word one way or the other. In fact, she'd repri- manded Trina for being unprofessional, and she'd clammed up when he'd asked her about being in a relationship.

Her vibes all said *back off*. And he didn't need to be paranormal to feel the message, so maybe he'd just have to accept that.

He had plenty on his plate without complicating things with a relationship. Still, something about her spoke to him, and he didn't understand it.

Nina and Marty looked at each other before Nina said, "She's fucking ripped, but she refused to come back here and chill out. Said she had to make sure all the data she's got on you is somewhere safe. So Darnell's in the lab with her right now, looking out for her while it gets cleaned up. Because, you know, you broke a fucking water tank with thousands of gallons of water in it."

Fuck. He sure had. "Damn. Again, I'm sorry, Marty. Just let me get Janet fed and I'll go over to Bobby-Sue and help clean up."

But Marty shook her head. "Nope. We've got it covered, and you have thank you cards to send," she teased.

"So, you wanna go look at your goodies? The were-bears sent a shit-ton of all kinds of berries and a gift certificate for some salmon company. You would not believe the damn size of the basket the dragons sent. Jesus, we could hardly get it in the door." Tapping the bed, Nina called to Janet. "C'mon, Sweet Pea. Auntie Nina has a steak bone just for you."

Janet's ears stood up and she instantly followed Nina out the bedroom door, leaving him with Marty.

"Is Scotty really okay?" She'd scared the shit out of him when she'd coughed so hard, he thought her lungs were going to pop right out of her mouth.

That was something he didn't get, either. He smelled something about her—something he didn't understand any more than he did when he'd smelled whatever had set him off in the tank.

"You like her, don't you?" Marty softly pointed out, tucking her gleaming hair behind her ears.

"I hardly know her," he protested.

She shrugged and winked. "Doesn't mean you can't have an instant attraction. Chemistry is chemistry. There are no rules when it comes to the laws of attraction."

Clearing his throat, Kash didn't say anything. Instead, he offered his arm. "C'mon. Let's go see what Supernatural Santa and his paranormal elves brought me, huh?"

Marty laughed, driving her hand through the crook of his arm. "Ooo, I hope the dragons sent ketchup."

He stopped short, his brow furrowing. "Ketchup?"

"Yeah, haven't you heard the old joke? Don't meddle in the affairs of dragons, because humans are crunchy and taste good with ketchup."

He began to laugh, but then he stopped. "Wait, am I going to want to eat humans?"

Marty winced with a giggle and pulled him out the door. "That's a conversation for another day."

Aw, hell...

AFTER SORTING through his gift baskets, Kash decided to take a minute to himself, maybe walk Janet. She'd love the snow out in the forest, where she could run freely without the constraints of a fence.

The house was quiet with most everyone off doing their thing, the way it always was this time of day, but for Darnell who sat in the living room in the chair by the fire, reading to Carl. So Kash grabbed Janet's harness and leash from the laundry room and put them on her.

Her excitement at going for a walk after several days without one was palpable. She wriggled and jumped around, her tongue flapping at his hands as he tried to get her to settle.

"Chill, little lady," he ordered, hooking the leash to her harness and walking her out to the living room. "Hey, guys, I'm gonna take Janet for a walk. If you need me, text me. I've got my phone."

Darnell leaned forward on the puffy camel-colored chair and smiled warmly. "Miss Janet needs some one-on-one time, for sure, don'tcha, pretty girl?" He shook his finger at Kash. "You be careful, ya hear? Don't go far and stay where I can smell ya."

"Be...safe, pl...ease. Please," Carl insisted with his crooked smile, giving Janet a scratch to her ears.

"And when you arrive back from your walk, I shall have freshly baked cookies and hot chocolate just for you, Master Kash, and maybe a little something for Mistress Janet," Arch called from the kitchen with a smile, smoothing back his tuft of blue hair.

Man, if these people were part of a cult, he'd lucked out as far as sects go. What cult baked you cookies and stuffed you with meal after sumptuous meal until you almost burst?

He smiled his gratitude. "Thanks, Arch, that's really nice of you."

"My pleasure. See you in a bit."

He flapped a hand over his shoulder and headed out the antique wood front door.

It was definitely cold out. He saw his breath, as sporadic as that was, but he didn't feel frigid the way it should if the thermometer outside was accurate. Not even a little.

Janet, on the other hand, didn't care how cold it was. She plowed into the snow, burying her nose.

Kash laughed. It felt good to do something normal with her. "Easy there, little lady. Don't spend your energy all at once."

Without warning, she took off through the yard, her strong legs pumping so fast, under human circumstances he wouldn't have been able to keep up, but as a newly minted paranormal? It was a breeze.

She headed through the open back gate and straight toward the woods, tugging and pulling, and even though she knew better, Kash didn't have the heart to correct her.

As quickly as she'd taken off was as quickly as she stopped short, her nose in the air, taking deep whiffs.

Nina popped out of the edge of the woods, her tall, willowy frame approaching them, her glossy black hair falling in long waves out of the hood on her jacket.

"Hey, guys!" she called, waving her hand to encourage them to come toward her, a smile on her pale face.

Kash waved back and began to head her way, but Janet was suddenly quite tentative. She refused to move. "What's the matter, Janet? It's Nina. Your favorite person."

As Nina moved toward them, her long legs crunching in the hard-packed snow, Janet's tail shot up in the air and the fur on her back stood on end.

He tried to tug her forward, but again she wouldn't move.

Nina patted her thighs with lean hands. "C'mere, doggie. C'mon," she said with a smile.

And that was when Kash knew something was off. First, he smelled it, and then he recognized it in the vampire's words and her smile.

Nina never called Janet *doggie*—not in the entire week he'd been here—and she rarely smiled at him unless it was in maniacal glee when she was busting his chops.

A smile from Nina was like a gift from above.

That's what cinched the deal for Kash. And the vampire had all sorts of pet names for Janet, but doggie definitely wasn't one of them.

It was too bad he didn't listen to his instincts sooner.

It might have saved him from being knocked out cold.

THIRTEEN

"I don't know who the fuck you are, but I'm gonna catch your fucking ass and when I do, Hell's gonna sound like a trip to fucking Chuck E. Cheese!"

Kash heard Nina's very scary threat, felt Scotty's hands on his forehead, brushing his hair from his face, but he didn't know what the hell had just happened.

"Kash! Oh my God, Kash, are you all right?" Scotty breathed with heaving gusts that fanned his cheeks. She pried his eye open, allowing him to see Marty on her knees at his other side, with Wanda beside her.

"We have to get him out of the snow," Wanda said, her hair, usually neatly up behind her head, falling around her face and lashing at her pink cheeks.

Marty looked to Wanda with worried eyes, her lips a thin line of raspberry lip gloss. "I'm going after the son of a bitch! Do you two have him or do you need my help?"

"We're fine—go!" Wanda yelled, grabbing Kash by the arm and preparing to haul him to his feet, but he almost couldn't help her for how battered he felt.

As his eyes cleared, he saw Marty take off so fast, she left ruts in the snow.

"Janet? Where's Janet?" he croaked, trying to sit up, but his back ached.

He couldn't lose Janet. He couldn't...

WHEN SCOTTY'D heard all the commotion, she'd come flying outside to see what was going on. Seeing Kash crumbled in the snow was almost her undoing.

Now, seeing him so pale, she had to fight to keep her fear at bay and her hands from shaking. "Nina will find her, I promise. Just stay still so I can check you for injuries," Scotty said, her eyes roaming over his body, checking to see where or if he'd been hurt. She smoothed her freezing-cold hands over his stomach, fighting the urge to admire the flat surface.

But he grabbed her wrists, his hands covered in snow, his eyes wild. "I have to find Janet. She's every-thing to me. *Please!*"

As she looked into his eyes under the fading light of late afternoon, something shifted in her. She had no explanation for the feeling. She didn't even think she could describe it properly.

There was no word yet crafted for it—but the connection she briefly experienced from the touch of his hands existed.

It. Existed. With it came peace and a weird sense of belonging.

And that frightened her enough to fall back in the snow with a jolt, the cold powder seeping into her jeans.

Kash was up and running after Nina and Marty before she could blink an eye, calling Janet's name with the sound of fear in his voice.

She's everything to me... His words tore at her heart. She wanted to know why he felt that way.

"Scotty!" Wanda was at her side in seconds, lifting her up off the freezing-cold ground. "C'mon, honey. Let's get you inside and warmed up."

But she stood rooted to the ground, her legs shaky. "No. I want to help find Janet."

"You're in no condition to do any such thing," Wanda scolded, her serene beauty now filled with fire. "Now let me help you to the house or I'll carry you there myself."

Scotty knew she was right. She knew she was jeopardizing her health with the possibility of catching a cold, which always turned into pneumonia in her case, but she didn't like it.

She was so damn tired of being so damn tired.

When she'd been on her way back from the lab, Wanda the Babysitter in tow, she'd seen Kash running with Janet toward the edge of the woods, then she'd heard Janet yelp and snarl...

And she'd seen Nina grab the dog and literally launch her out of the way to make a run for Kash.

Both she and Wanda froze on the spot. Nina would just as soon make an idle threat as she would throw a dog.

They both knew something was horribly wrong, and when Darnell came barreling out of the house and sniffed the air. "Somethin's not right, Doc. You guys go get help!"

He took off running after Nina, who'd hauled Kash over her shoulder like a sack of potatoes and began running into the woods.

Scotty ran toward the guesthouse, her breathing choppy, her legs wobbly, but she made it just in time to see Marty arrive in her big SUV.

As she explained to them what she'd witnessed, Nina came flying out of the guesthouse door. What the hell was going on?

But she didn't have time to ask. They'd all run into the woods to find Kash, Scotty included, and found him dumped in a snowdrift just a few hundred feet in, passed out cold.

As Wanda helped her back to the house, she heard yelling from behind them. "Janet! C'mere, baby girl!

Auntie Nina's got treats!"

Wanda patted her on the shoulder. "Keep walking, young lady."

"But—"

Wanda gave her a firm nudge forward. "Nope. No buts. You've taken enough risks with your health today. We're not in the business of gambling here."

She steered her inside the door, where Arch greeted her with a heated blanket and something hot to drink. "Come sit by the fire with Master Carl, Doctor," he encouraged with a warm smile.

She allowed Wanda to lead her to the soft couch, where she dropped down and Carl began pulling her boots off.

"Thank you, Carl," she whispered, fighting the rush of tears.

Espy hopped up to the back of the couch, wrapping her tail around Scotty's neck and rubbing her soft cheek against her head. Intuitively, she knew Scotty needed her. She always knew.

The thought made her heart tighten. What the hell had happened out there, and why had someone who looked just like Nina attacked Kash?

And what if Janet didn't come back? What if someone hurt her? What if...

She clutched the mug's handle, scrunching her eyes shut.

Carl sat next to her on the couch and put his arm

around her, tucking the blanket around her legs. "You ooo...okay?"

She gave his hand a tender pat and nodded. God, he was the sweetest. "I'm fine, Carl. I'm just worried about Janet and Kash."

Wanda knelt in front of her, her eyes worried as she took Scotty's hand in hers, giving it a squeeze. "Are you okay? Really okay?"

She squeezed Wanda's hand in return, letting her fingers curl into her soft palm. "I swear, I'm fine. I just don't understand what happened."

"Can you tell me what you saw, honey? I was still lost in thought over the tank incident that I didn't pay any attention."

She shook her head in astonishment, still not sure what happened. "Nina. I saw Nina throw Janet out of her way, then grab Kash, toss him over her shoulder and run toward the woods. Why would she do that?"

Wanda's lips pursed, her words cautious. "She wouldn't. Not unless he did something to anger her. I think we both know that would never happen—not in this lifetime."

"But Janet... Janet was acting weird, too. She growled at her. Then when Darnell went after them, Nina came out of the house..." She paused a moment, then gripped Wanda's hand tighter as so many thoughts rushed through her brain with one standing out like a sore thumb. "Wait! Do you think..."

But wait. No. Really? Yes! It made sense. It made perfect sense.

Wanda tugged Scotty's hand, her eyes searching her face. "*What?* Do I think what?"

"I know this will sound crazy, but what is crazy anymore? Do you think that was a skinwalker?"

Wanda gasped, her eyes going wide. "That makes perfect sense, because Nina would never hurt any animal, and while she appears always annoyed by Kash, she's always annoyed by everyone. She'd never hurt a client. Not without a really good reason."

Scotty's head felt dizzy as her mind raced. "So why the heck is a skinwalker here? Is there a group of them in Buffalo that I'm unaware of? And if so, what do they want with Kash?"

Wanda jumped up and began to pace, clasping her hands together. "When you tested Kash to find out what his traits were, did you even think to test for a skinwalker?"

She blinked and cocked her head, biting the inside of her cheek before she said, "I didn't. It never occurred to me because he didn't exhibit any signs of a skinwalker."

God, how stupid could she be? This was one of many reasons she couldn't get involved with Kash. She lost all perspective thanks to his dreamy eyes and hot body.

Wanda snapped her fingers, her eyes gleaming.

"But that must be it, right? I mean, what else would explain someone who looks exactly like Nina?"

"But don't most skinwalkers shift into animals? I admit, I have zero experience with that particular faction of the paranormal. I wouldn't know what to look for to begin with, but I can tell you for sure, nothing I didn't recognize showed up in his blood tests."

Wanda nodded as she paced, her sensible but sophisticated shoes clacking on the hardwood. "There are some skinwalkers who can shift into human forms. Their ability isn't exclusive to animals. I don't know any, and I'm almost positive they're extremely rare and there are very few left. But all that aside, if that was a skinwalker, which feels like the only explanation, as you said, why do they want a piece of Kash?"

Scotty bit the inside of her cheek again, pulling the blanket tighter around her midsection. "I don't know. Everyone's been so nice. I mean, Nina and Marty texted me pics of all the gift baskets Kash got today from a bunch of different factions. It's an embarrassment of riches. Why wouldn't the skinwalkers be onboard, too?"

Wanda wrinkled her nose, narrowing her eyes. "Because you know as well as I do, some people, some of the *ancients* specifically, don't feel the way the newer order does. Maybe it just didn't show up in any of the blood tests? I mean, you have to admit, stranger things have been known to happen. Your mother, for instance. She's full vampire and she had a *human* baby. That's almost unheard of."

"That's fair. I may well have missed something." Scotty hated to admit it, but she was, after all, only *human.*

"Maybe Kash was bitten or scratched by a skinwalker at the bar and they want to take him out to ensure secrecy? It's the only explanation I can think of."

Scotty gulped. Not only did Kash have to worry about how all of his paranormal characteristics were going to pan out, he had to worry someone might try to harm him for something he had no control over?

There was a scratch at the door, then a low, shuddering whimper. Carl jumped up and ran to open the door, where Janet burst into the room, covered in snow and shivering.

"Janet!" Scotty cried, rising to greet her. "Thank God you're all right!"

She ran straight to Scotty, knocking her back to the couch. She wrapped her arms around Janet's neck and hugged her tight. "I'm so glad you're okay," she whispered against her wet fur, tears stinging her eyes.

Janet pushed her large body into Scotty's, almost as if she needed shielding from whatever was outside. The fear of something malevolent, waiting for them, lurking in the shadows, made her shiver

Arch rushed in with warm towels and dog treats

while Wanda texted Nina and Marty to let them know Janet was back.

But she needn't have bothered, Nina, Marty and a ragged-looking Kash followed quickly behind.

Kash rushed to the couch, dropping down and hauling Janet into his arms, stroking her back as Arch busied himself drying the dog's paws. "Jesus, little lady, are you okay?"

Janet buried her head in Kash's strong shoulder, making Scotty fight to keep her tears at bay.

She so desperately wanted to curl into them, add her warmth to theirs, become part of their bond and she had absolutely no explanation for why she felt this way. But it was so strong, so consuming, it burned in her gut as yearning clawed her from the inside out.

"What in all of heaven happened out there?" Wanda asked Kash while brushing snow clumps from Marty's hair.

"I don't know... I know I say that a lot these days, but I *really* don't know. I was taking Janet for a walk and I swear, I thought that was Nina until she smiled at me. I should have made a run for it right that second."

Nina flicked his shoulder, shaking her hair free of snow and purposely dumping it on Kash. "Fuck you, Burgermeister. I damn well smile."

He gave her a look of mock astonishment as he brushed snow from his jeans. "Not at me, you don't, and to top it off, you—or *fake* you—called Janet 'doggie.' You've never called her doggie. Next thing I know, fake Nina's thrown Janet out of the way, rushing at me and launching me over her shoulder like I don't weigh over two-hundred pounds, and then everything went black. Swear to Christ, I've never been knocked out so often as I have since I met you guys."

Scotty turned on the couch to look at Kash, his pink hair dripping, his fangs now fully exposed and almost normal, his right eye black and blue. "Are you all right? Do you feel light-headed? Dizzy?"

He groaned and rubbed the back of his neck with the palm of his normal hand. "I feel like I was hit by a moving truck. Whoever grabbed me wasn't a wimp, but I'm mostly fine."

"So what the fuck is happening here?" Nina asked Wanda, pulling off her wet hoodie to hang it by the door. "Who the hell is pretending to be me, and why?"

Darnell stomped in just then, huffing and puffing. He leaned forward and put his hands on his knees to catch his breath.

Nina clapped him on the back, an expression of concern on her face. "Dude, you okay?"

Darnell bobbed his head, pulling off his knit cap. "I followed until I lost the scent. I dunno what that was, but it fo' sure wasn't anything I ever smelled before today, and believe you me, I've smelled some stuff."

Both Nina and Marty nodded their agreement, their faces grim. "Same," Marty offered, accepting a towel from Arch with a grateful smile. "I've never smelled such an unusual scent before."

Kash ran a hand over his hair. "So can any of you explain what just happened? Why would someone want to kidnap me?"

Nina cracked her fingers. "You did hear the part about the bad people, didn't you, Burgermeister? We told you shit like this happens, right?"

He licked his lips and ran a hand over his weary face, giving it a scrub with his palm. "You did. Now I want to know what it was. Who has the ability to make themselves look like another person? Because I'm telling you, whoever that was looked just like Nina. *Exactly* like Nina. Janet noticed it wasn't her first, which is why I guess she was snarling and growling at her, but it took me a minute to get the bigger picture."

Scotty put her hand on his arm without thinking, relishing the warmth that flooded through her veins. "We're only guessing at this point, but something called a skinwalker has the ability to shapeshift into animals and people."

Kash frowned in obvious confusion. "A what now?"

"Skinwalker!" Nina shouted, making Janet jump. "Mother of all fucks! That makes sense. But if that was a skinwalker, what the shit do they want with him? He can't shift into other people or animals."

"Yet," Scotty muttered. "Wanda suggested maybe he was bitten or scratched by a skinwalker and we don't know it. Maybe they know something we don't and sent someone to eliminate the problem altogether without bothering to ask questions first. I didn't test Kash's blood for that characteristic because there was nothing that suggested he was a skinwalker. But that doesn't mean it won't crop up at a later date. That's what this whole moving-into-the-guesthouse is about. Discovery."

Wanda brushed her hands together in a "no more of this nonsense" fashion, her eyes on fire, her index finger waving in the air. "Well, that does it then. As of right now, Kash goes nowhere without at least one of the four of us. Neither does Scotty. I'm going to get in touch with the council and see what I can find out about skinwalkers and whether they have someone who's in charge—and if they do, you can bet your sweet bupkiss there will be words, and they'll be unkind. Maybe even ugly. I won't have this sort of blatant display of stupidity from any faction—not while I'm around."

Nina pinched Wanda's crimson cheek and chuckled. "I love when Mama Bear gets bent out of shape."

Giving Janet one last kiss on the top of her head, Scotty rose from the couch, her legs much less shaky. "I'm going back to the lab to look at Kash's blood test results so you'll have all the information you need when you speak to whoever's in charge, Wanda."

But Nina held up a hand, grabbing her by the jaw and tilting her head upward, examining her face. "You feel all right? You were hacking pretty good out there. I don't want you getting fucking sick on top of the rest of this nutty shit."

Scotty brushed her hands away. "I'm fine. Coughing comes with what's wrong—" She stopped abruptly, shaking her head and pursing her lips. "I'm fine. Really. It won't take but a few minutes anyway, then I'll come right back here, have some dinner, and get a good night's rest, okay, Marshmallow?"

"Fuck you," Nina retorted with a grin. "Wait right there. Lemme get a dry jacket and I'll take you."

Kash got up off the couch, tucking the blanket around Janet, who Carl came and sat near to keep her calm. "I'll come, too."

"No!" Scotty gulped, swallowing how quickly she'd reacted. She didn't want to be in the lab with him. Not feeling the way she felt about him in the woods and on the couch. It was too intense. Too over-whelming. "I mean, *no*. It's okay. You should rest. You just had a traumatic experience. Rest is needed. Doctor's orders," she attempted to tease.

"They're my test results, right? I'd kinda like to be there if I'm going to find out I'm a skin-whatever," he argued stubbornly.

"Skin*walker*, dumbass. Now both of you, shut up and let's go. I gotta Skype with my man and my kid in an hour. And you," she jabbed Kash in the arm, "no more recreating Niagara Falls. Got it?" She pointed toward the door. "March."

Kash smiled at her. "You bet, Marshmallow."

Scotty couldn't help but laugh out loud at Kash's gall.

It was either that or cry.

The idea of being in the lab with Kash suddenly felt very intimate, but maybe having Nina with them would help ease her discomfort.

Maybe.

FOURTEEN

O r not.

Nina opted to sit outside the lab, where some of the workers Marty had sent in to clean up had put the treadmill and much of the other lab equipment.

She said she could keep better watch if she was able see all angles, and seeing as the lab was windowless, there wasn't any other way in but through the halls of the basement.

Reluctantly, Scotty flipped on the lights with Kash in tow, his booted feet clomping behind her. His cologne wafting to her nose, mingling with the lingering scent of chlorine, his presence ever looming.

She pointed to the lone chair that hadn't been swept away by the tank's water. "Sit there and wait while I go over your results again."

He sighed, his big chest expanding as he traipsed over to the chair and plunked down. "You're the boss."

"I am," she replied, rather petulantly. Now, if she could simply ignore him and the strange and over-whelming feeling he'd evoked in her while in the woods and at the guesthouse, all would be well.

She could go back to the guesthouse, have dinner with everyone the way she had every night this week and make it an early night.

Distance was crucial. If she could continue to create some the way she had all week long, she'd be just fine.

But when Scotty turned around, his chart in hand, Kash once more stood right behind her, taking up all the space and smelling so good, she had to grit her teeth.

"I told you to sit," she said stiffly.

He chuckled, deep and low, sending shivers along her arms. "I didn't realize I was under arrest. Can't I see *my* file?"

Her nose almost brushed his chest, he was so close. Taking a step back, Scotty inhaled a deep, cleansing breath, reminding herself to remain profes-sional and not behave like some horny high schooler. Maybe a cockier approach was necessary?

"Would you even understand what all these numbers meant if I shared them?"

He shrugged his wide shoulders. "I took chemistry in high school. I know...stuff."

"Stuff? You need to know more than just *stuff*." With a sigh, she moved away from him and back to what was left of her desk and the things she'd managed to save. A tumbled mess of papers, reports, her computer and a microscope. "You need to know a lot more *stuff* than your eighth-grade science teacher taught you. This involves years of schooling."

"My eighth-grade science teacher was awesome," he murmured. "Mr. Campanella. Great guy. I hated when I had to leave his class."

"Why did you have to leave?" Scotty asked before she could stop herself. *Damnit, Scotty. Shut up.*

"New fosters," he explained. "I had plenty of them."

How sad. She was always complaining about her parents, but they'd given her a stable home and plenty of love, despite their disappointment in her lack of paranormal abilities. Her heart ached for twelve-year-old Kash and his brother.

She turned to look at him, and once again found him but a foot away. His broad shoulders, muscled and firm, came to just above her nose and she had to fight tooth and nail not to reach out and run a hand over them.

Licking her dry lips, Scotty forced herself to stay relaxed. Doctors talked to their patients about their lives all the time to engage them, to remind them they were interested in them as human beings. She just had to remember to draw the line before it went too far.

She could do that. She *would* do that.

"So you moved around a lot?" Scotty pretended to look at his charts even though she saw nothing but lines and dots. She lost all focus and reason when Kash was near.

"I was in foster care since around the age of five, and my brother Garrick was two."

Scotty literally gasped out loud, then clamped a hand over her mouth, her chest tight. The word "why" spilled out of her mouth before she could prevent her lips from forming the question.

He shoved his hands into the pockets of his jeans and shrugged. "I don't remember a lot about when we were taken from my mother. I only remember some of it. Needles and paraphernalia of that nature were always all over the place. She was a junkie, and because of that, she couldn't get us back. After we were taken, I never saw her again. Died sometime in the late nineties, I think. Oddly, what I mostly remember from that time in my life was how hungry I was and how Garrick always had a wet, saggy diaper."

She was no psychologist, but his fear of needles could certainly be explained with memories of that nature.

Instinctively, Scotty reached a hand out and placed it on his arm, her throat dry, her heart filled with sorrow. "Oh, Kash, how awful for you both."

He gave her a half smile, crooked and endearing. "Much like you, I don't want anyone to feel sorry for me. It happened. It's over. I survived." Kash paused and looked down at her, his amber eyes serious. "Nay. I *thrived*. So did Garrick."

Scotty studied his gorgeous face, obsessed with the dimples on either side of his mouth. "Sorry about that. But if I didn't feel something akin to deep sorrow for two small boys left to the system, I'd be a real asshole. I can't imagine being so young and shuffled off to a strange place with strange people."

"Ten homes in thirteen years. We moved a lot, but we had a great caseworker named Miss Meg—who I still keep in touch with, by the way—and she tried like hell to keep the two of us together."

"*Ten?*" she breathed in horror. "Why so often?"

Kash shrugged again, almost as if it was a defense mechanism—one she could certainly relate to. "Because two children were harder to place, and at first, they mostly only wanted Garrick because he was a toddler. But our caseworker was determined to keep us together. So we bounced around a lot, except for the six months Garrick spent in juvie."

Now she smiled up at him, and teased, "I would have thought you were the troublemaker, but it was your brother, huh?"

"Hah! Garrick was always into something. He was the risk-taker and I was the cautious one. I was always afraid we'd be kicked out of our foster home, and Garrick didn't give a rat's ass. At least not until he spent time in juvie."

"So you were never adopted? Either of you?"

His look was one of sadness, but it was brief before he put that smile back on his face. "Nope. I aged out of the system at eighteen, got a steady job, and with the help of Miss Meg, got a state-assisted apartment and custody of Garrick."

Scotty's eyes went wide, mostly with admiration. "So you raised him until he was eighteen when you were still just a kid yourself?" He wasn't only incredible-looking; he was a good person who loved animals and took care of his brother.

Damn.

Kash's glance at her was sheepish. "I did. It wasn't easy. Especially seeing as he was in juvie. It was important he not get into any more trouble until the state released him from foster care. Keeping him on the straight and narrow from sixteen to seventeen gave me a whole new respect for parents everywhere."

She tipped her head back and laughed, remembering how rebellious she was at that age—mostly due in part to her illness and her parents' overprotective nature. "I'm sure my folks would agree."

With a deep chuckle that slithered along her entire body, making it glow, he asked, "Was Dr. Scotty a bad teenager? I can't believe that. You're always so serious and focused."

She rolled her eyes at him, taking a shaky breath, suddenly feeling exposed and vulnerable. "I wasn't *bad*-bad. I tested the limits. Nothing big. Breaking curfew, a little underage drinking. You know, the norm. It only lasted for six months or so before I realized I was jeopardizing my grades, and really what I wanted was to get the hell away from my parents and live my life. But doesn't everyone at that age?"

Oh, the disagreements she'd had with her parents over going to college. They, or maybe more specifically, her father, wanted her to attend a college close to home to keep her safe and her medical needs in check, and she wanted to go to the ends of the opposite side of the Earth to get out from under their thumb.

Looking back now, their arguments felt silly compared to Kash's life. He'd been raising a fifteen-year-old at eighteen, while she'd been deciding what color sheets she wanted for her dorm room.

It made her feel like a spoiled, entitled brat.

His deep voice cut into her thoughts. "So... speaking of your parents...they're vampires. What the hell was that like growing up and why didn't they turn you? Color me fascinated."

Crossing her arms over her chest, Scotty lifted an eyebrow and gave him a crooked smile. "They didn't *ever* try to turn me, but you can believe *I* sure tried to get turned. But as much as you're an anomaly, I am, too. It just so happens; I can't be turned."

Kash whistled with clear astonishment. "Wait, so you let someone bite you? On purpose?"

"Bite, scratch, etcetera. Nothing's ever worked, and as Nina and crew have told you, biting someone can come with severe punishment in this new era of para-normal, so for sure my parents wouldn't agree to do something like that. They claim to love me just the way I am."

"And you don't believe that?"

She was starting to wonder *what* she believed. She'd always thought her parents found her a disap-pointment, but after hearing Kash's story, maybe that was her own insecurity talking.

Yes, her father believed in keeping up appearances and doing him proud, but was it because she had to work harder, seeing as she was human? Or had that simply been her perception?

"I believe they did the best they knew how to do with a daughter who didn't have their capabilities. We were apples and oranges."

"So did you grow up with other humans?"

"Oh, sure. There were humans in my life. Someone had to feed me real food, right?" she said on a chuckle. "I always wondered what it'd be like to have parents who couldn't read my mind, or to lift a pickup truck with nothing but a finger."

Kash's mouth fell open. "Your parents can lift a pickup truck? I mean, I know vampires are strong because, well, *Nina*. But a truck? Full-size?"

She nodded with a giggle. "Four-door extended cab."

Kash whistled his admiration. "Shut the front door."

Scotty snickered, only just this second realizing how much closer they were standing. Yet, she didn't move. She couldn't. She was incapable of moving away from the warmth of his very being.

"I lost an earring in our driveway when I was in high school, so my father helped me look for it by picking up his truck." She shook off the memory and tried to focus. "Anyway...I thought I had it rough. But now, looking back, I had it great compared to you and your brother. In fact, I feel like an ass for ever complaining about my folks."

"Nah. Don't. We managed and came out on top."

"I'll say you did, Burgermeister. You're a successful business owner and semi-retired at forty. Well done, you."

His lips thinned when he nodded. "And now I'm paranormal gumbo with no idea what's going to happen next."

Scotty thought about that before she responded with a teasing, "Do we ever know what's going to happen next?"

"Do we ever expect what's going to happen next might involve a tail or fangs and pink hair?"

She laughed out loud. "Valid point."

The door popped open and Nina stuck her beautiful face inside. "Excuse me, Romeo and Juliet, it sounds like you're havin' a laugh-riot in here and that's great. I'm glad you're getting to know each other. Really." She pounded her chest where her heart should be. "I'm gettin' all the feels. But here's the thing, stop dicking around playing flirty-flirt and get a move on. I have shit to do. Understood?"

"We weren't flirting," she protested, maybe a little too quickly.

But Nina's face hardened. "I said, *understood*?"

Scotty immediately straightened, squaring her shoulders. "Understood."

Kash saluted her, clicking his heels together. "Sir, yes, sir."

She narrowed her eyes at him and shook a finger in his direction. "That's yes, Dark Mistress, thank you very fucking much."

Kash began to laugh but when the vampire glared at him in disapproval, he instantly zipped his lip.

She closed the door, leaving them both fighting more laugher before Scotty caught herself and shook it off.

Nina was right. She'd been flirting with Kash and no matter how irresistible, that was unacceptable. The intimacy she was feeling was a hard no, and she knew it.

With a stern point of her finger in the direction of the chair, Scotty said, "Go sit and be quiet and let me look at these tests again before we get into real trouble with Crabby Patty. I need to concentrate, and I can't do that with you looking over my shoulder."

He made a comically big deal of tiptoeing over to

the chair and plopping down in it, but he was still smiling.

By some miracle, the vials of Kash's blood hadn't been swept away by the tank break. They were safely stored on shelves on the wall, and she was going to need them because flipping through his charts, Scotty saw nothing that would indicate skinwalker. Nothing.

Rather than put him through another round of needles, she decided to use the blood sample they'd taken this afternoon before she began to run more tests.

"Anything?" he asked, crossing his ankles, the fin that still stuck out flopping as he did.

She went to the microscope and grabbed a slide. "I'm just going to run a quick test with the sample we took this afternoon before this all happened. Outwardly, it doesn't look like anything has changed, so I don't need another sample from you."

Kash exhaled, as though relieved. He didn't show how much he hated blood and needles, but there was no hiding it from her practiced eyes. Now that she had some of his backstory, she'd remember to be sensitive to that particular detail.

Patting herself on the back, she set the slide under the microscope and put a drop of Kash's blood on it.

See, Scotty? You can personalize someone's care without getting in too deep. Good on you.

Scotty was so busy patting herself on the back, she

didn't see the tiny shard of glass on the edge of her desk, likely from the exploding water tank. When she reached for her glasses, it caught her, nicking her fingertip.

"Damn it!" Due to the medication she took for her disease, her blood was thin, with plenty to spare—which meant it dripped all over everything.

Including the slide under the scope.

Kash was up and out of his chair before she could stop him, grabbing a tissue box on a nearby shelf. "You okay?"

Taking the tissue, she flapped her hand at him, irritated with herself and her stupid limitations. "I'm fine. Your blood sample? Not so much. I've ruined it."

He rolled up the sleeve of his sweater. "You need more?"

Pressing the tissue to her finger, she moved around his big body and shook her head. "No. I collected plenty from you this morning. No worries."

Glancing down at the microscope, preparing to put a fresh sample in the tainted slide's place, she gasped, her eyes going wide.

"Now what?" he asked in a teasing tone, hands on his hips. "Am I gonna turn into a werechicken? Grow a waddle? Cluck?"

But she was too astonished to even laugh at his joke. Moving her head slowly in negative fashion, Scotty grabbed her glasses, pushed them over her nose and looked at the slide under the microscope.

What in all of paranormal batshittery was happening?

He must have sensed her surprise. Taking her by the shoulders, Kash spun her around to look at him. "*What?* What are you seeing? You're kinda freaking me out here, Scotty."

Licking her dry lips, Scotty forced herself to form words. "Your blood..."

Kash cocked his head, eyebrow raised. "Uh-huh. What about it?"

"I cut myself. It dripped on the slide by accident..."

"And?"

"And your blood, mixed with mine, stops your blood from changing." *Holy hell.*

"I don't understand. Our blood mixed together means what in layman's terms?"

She gripped his arms, forgetting her plan to create distance between them. "As a paranormal, your blood is very different from a human's, but mixed with my human blood, it..."

"It what?" he asked stiffly, staring down at her.

Scotty blinked. "It becomes human again."

Holy, holy shit.

CHAPTER

FIFTEEN

K ash wasn't sure what to say. He'd been trying to find the words since Scotty's discovery, but they wouldn't come.

Go figure. It appeared, in times of extreme stress, like when one finds out they're paranormal times ten, one shuts down. He'd definitely shut down. His loss for words was becoming legendary.

She'd given as thorough an explanation as possible. Her human red blood cells had seemingly attacked his paranormal blood cells.

Because Scotty was immune to becoming paranormal, her blood somehow acted as an anti-body to his paranormalness—or whatever they called what he'd turned into.

Kash had been both riveted and horrified by the information, and it had all become too much to digest.

Now, they all sat at the dinner table, overwhelmed.

And despite the fact that they'd essentially discovered something so enormous it could alter his life yet again, Kash's appetite didn't seem to care.

He shoveled mountains of fluffy mashed potatoes and a rare porterhouse down his gullet like he'd never eat again. It was easier to keep eating rather than try and form a complete sentence.

So he let everyone around him talk while he ate buckets of rich, buttery corn.

"So what the fuck does this mean, Doc?" Nina asked, tilting the dining room chair back with her feet. "Can he go back to being human with something like a damn blood transfusion?"

Scotty wiped her mouth and gave them all a look that said she had no idea. "I don't think it's as simple as that, Nina. I mean, there are a million of things to take into consideration. First, I don't think I could personally withstand a transfusion. Not with—"

She stopped short again, the exact way she had when he'd wanted to come to the lab with her earlier, and Kash wanted to know what she was keeping from him.

But he couldn't ask because his mouth was full. So he kept chewing.

Wanda repositioned the charcoal-gray napkin in her lap. "So no transfusion."

Scotty shook her dark head, her shiny hair falling around her shoulders. "No transfusions—for now, anyway. I don't know what a full transfusion of human blood would do to him. He doesn't need a blood transfusion. But I also don't understand how my blood, of all the blood in the land, could reverse his condition. It's something I've never heard of. Never even thought about. I *do* know, we have to keep this very quiet. We don't need a bunch of people sniffing around and jumping the gun before things have been tested and retested."

Marty put her arms on the table and steepled her hands under her chin. "Do you think this is going to be another one of those paranormal anomalies we can't explain? Are we just going to chalk it up to another magical, paranormal wonder?"

Scotty chewed a piece of steak and swallowed, her expression still filled with confusion. "I don't know. I just know it happened. I triple checked. It makes no sense, but it happened. I don't know what good it does to have this information, but I know I've never seen anything so incredible."

Kash shoveled more mashed potatoes into his face, savoring the creamy texture, as Wanda reached over and rubbed his back. "Hey, you okay there? No one's asked you how *you* feel about this."

Swallowing, he shrugged his shoulders. "What *should* I feel about it? If it doesn't mean I can go back to being human, nothing changes for me."

Scotty set her fork down and looked at him, her eyes scanning his. "You're right. I can't say for sure it means anything other than our blood mixed together makes human blood, but this needs to be researched. Maybe it's not just my blood that can do this. Maybe, somewhere down the road, we can figure out how to turn a paranormal accident back into a human."

Marty blew out a puff of air and leaned back in her chair. "I don't even know what that would be like anymore. I've been a were for over fifteen years. I'm sorta used to the shift and buying razors in bulk."

Wanda let her chin rest on her fist. "I know for sure I wouldn't go back. Not because of my abilities, but because I love my life just the way it is. I wouldn't change a darn thing."

"Well, I did go back for a little while," Nina reminded them, her eyes glittering. "It was fucking great to eat chicken wings and whatever again, but thinking Charlie and Carl and Greg and all you guys would outlive me? That shit hurt my fucking soul. I'll stay a vampire, thanks."

Where he didn't have words a few moments ago, Kash quite suddenly found them, and they were angry.

"You know why that is, ladies? Because you don't look like sideshow freaks. You have cool side-affects like teeth that are sharp and pointy, not hanging out of your head, making you look like you've never been to a dentist. You can shift into a big, scary werewolf who runs fast and is a sci-fi dream come true. I, on the other hand, have pink hair, a half-assed fin, an even bigger half-assed wing, some teeth that only come out to play occasionally and a scruffy tail we have to tape to my back. I have a damn *tail.* Is there anyone else in the paranormal world who looks like me?"

"No," Marty whispered softly, her eyes round and full of concern.

"Then I'm a freak in both the human and the paranormal world. That's awesome," he spat, his anger spiking.

Kash pushed the chair away from the dining room table and glared at them.

Marty was the first to offer him sympathy he didn't want. "You're experiencing a shift in emotion, Kash. Remember what I said. You have to recognize it and rein it in."

Lobbing his napkin on the table, Kash frowned. "So I can't ever get angry? Werewolves don't get angry? Aren't you angry when you're eating small, woodland creatures or sucking the life out of someone through their necks?"

Nina was in his face in seconds, her pale skin glowing by the light coming from the fireplace. "Back the fuck off, Burgermeister. I don't suck the life out of anyone. Now pay close attention. You can get angry, motherfucker. You can't get angry with *us.* Got that? We didn't do this to you. Check that shit or I'll check it for you."

"Kash," Scotty said, trying to keep her tone reassuring but even. "I know this is upsetting. I know having all these things happen to your body is overwhelming, but we just need to give it time. I'm convinced if we wait this out, we'll be able to force your abilities to make an appearance and all of your physical abnormalities will ease."

Kash's jaw went tight and he had to take deep breaths to keep from throwing something. His anger rose and fell like the swell of high tide.

Darnell put a hand on his shoulder. His really big hand. Kash wasn't sure if it was in warning or comfort, but he made his presence known.

"C'mon, man. Let's go for a walk and cool off."

Instantly, the ugly red haze consuming Kash's thoughts eased and he realized what a petty jerkoff he was being.

Marty was right. None of this was their fault. He was the idiot who'd gone into a bar called NOPE.

Kash took a deep breath, immediately remorseful. He looked them all in the eye. "That sounds like a good idea, Darnell. I'm sorry, ladies. You too, Carl. I just..." He never seemed to be able to finish that sentence, but he absolutely was sorry.

All the women and Carl gave him looks of sympathy he didn't deserve. Instead of making things worse, he opted to let Darnell lead him outside.

When they stepped out onto the small front porch, the snow fell in thick sheets, but Kash didn't care, he walked out into the center of it, letting the cool flecks pelt his hot face.

Darnell followed behind him, clapping him on the

back. "This ain't easy, I know. Cain't say as I blame ya for bein' so mad."

He shook his head, more remorseful than ever. "It's still no excuse to be abusive. I have to try harder to control it. I guess this whole blood thing caught me off guard. I realize it's probably years away from being useful, but hearing it could reverse the effects of a bite gave me two seconds of hope."

Darnell nodded and began walking down the drive, his large body moving surprisingly swiftly for someone so big. "This gig can be really unfair. Don't I know it. You always gotta be careful around humans. Cain't let 'em see the real you. You always gotta watch your back. But I'm here to tell ya, you couldn't have walked into it with better people than them three in there. You got a right to be frustrated and angry about how much your life's gonna change, Kash, but there's some positives to this, too."

Kash said nothing. He didn't want to be an asshole again, but he was hard-pressed to find a positive.

The light from the line of lanterns illuminating the path of the driveway glowed on Darnell's pleasantly round face. "Am I right in sayin' you only have a brother? Nobody else?"

Kash stopped walking, swishing his feet in the snow. "That's right. It's just us. Why do you ask?"

His lips tilted up at the corners as he rocked back on his high tops. "'Cause now you have a whole family of people who got your back. It ain't just you and your brother no more, buddy. That's a pretty big positive, if ya ask me. "Course, what do I know. I been a demon forever. I do know, those women back there gave me a purpose when I had none. They included me. They loved me when nobody else did. That means somethin' to old Darnell."

Kash's jaw loosened and his chest released the stress tension he was feeling. Damn Darnell for making him see the good stuff. "I feel like an ass."

"You was," he said on a deep, hearty chuckle. "But you won't always be. I'll help you with the shift. Maybe all we gotta do is take some time to teach you how to do it."

As his anger dissipated, he began to feel less murderous. "There's a skill to it? It doesn't just happen?"

"Nope. It doesn't always just happen. You can ask Miss Marty in there about the struggle she had shifting into her werewolf form. Took a little bit. The way she tells it, it was bad enough she had all these emotional swings happenin', and not being able to change into her new form left her feeling like the biggest outcast ever."

Kash clucked his tongue and stared into the dark velvet of the night. "I guess it makes me feel a little less like a failure. Though, it's hard to imagine Marty failing. Not after what I saw her do shortly after I met her."

Darnell grinned, his smile lighting up his whole

face. "Oh, she's real good at it now. But see? It can happen. She says, all you gotta do is learn to concentrate and visualize. Me and Carl can help. You wanna try tomorrow after lunch?"

Closing his eyes, he let the snow soothe him and the frigid wind wash over his heated limbs. "That would be amazing. If Dr. Frankenstein in there will give me some time off, I'm in."

"Hey!" a voice from behind them chimed. "Stop making it sound like I'm Attila the Research Scientist. And if you must call me names, I prefer Madame Curie."

Darnell and Kash both laughed as Scotty approached them with a very happy Janet in tow.

Janet rubbed up against him, swatting him with her backend. "Sorry. If *Madame Curie* will let me have a little time off as her guinea pig, I'm happy to try and figure out this shifting thing, Darnell."

Scotty's eyes twinkled playfully. "Oooo, you have a date with a demon. That's awesome. Now, c'mon. Let's walk Janet. She could use a good leg stretch."

Normally he'd be thrilled to spend more time with Scotty, but Kash was worried about her health. He didn't know what, because no one would tell him what was going on with her—and there was definitely something wrong—but beyond that, she was so petite, he feared the wind might pick her up and carry her off.

"It's pretty cold out here. Maybe that's not a good idea."

But she handed him Janet's leash and put her arm through his. "I've lived in Buffalo and its surrounding areas all my life. The cold never bothers me. I love it and I love winter. So let's walk. Janet has to potty."

Darnell put his arms around both of them. "I'm gonna stay right behind y'all to be safe. Don't get out of my eyesight, ya hear?"

"I hear and I obey. Now let's do this, Burgermeister," Scotty said cheerfully.

Had she been replaced by one of those skinwalkers? Why was she suddenly all rainbows and soft fuzzy kittens?

As they changed course and began to move toward the woods, Kash glanced at her under the moonlight, her cheeks pink from the cold and covered in snowflakes, her dark hair hanging down the sides of her face beneath a red knit cap.

"What's gotten into you?"

"I don't know what you mean."

"You do, too. Suddenly you actually want to be in my company?"

She grinned. "*Janet* wanted to be in your company."

"You could have let Nina bring her to me."

"She didn't ask Nina to go potty. She asked me."

"She really likes you."

"And I really like her."

She just didn't really like *him*. Not the way he liked her anyway.

"So where do we go from here, Scotty? What's next on my paranormal plate?"

Stopping by a mountain of a bare-limbed maple encrusted in ice, she looked up at him, leaning her back against the tree. "Listen. I shouldn't have blurted that information out because it doesn't really mean anything right now anyway, and I'm sorry I was so unprofessional about it. I was just so shocked. Nothing like that has ever happened, and I'm usually alone in the lab when and if I make discoveries."

He was over the whole incident now and feeling a bit more hopeful. "You were excited. I get it. I shouldn't have jumped to conclusions I know are unrealistic."

"For now, it would be crazy to think I could just pump some of my blood into you and turn you back into a human. The test slide had only a couple of drops of blood. Not pints. That's not how transfusions work, Kash. You don't give blood to an otherwise healthy body that doesn't need a transfusion anyway. And you are mostly healthy despite your new traits making everything so wonky. And even if this is some kind of crazy antidote, formulating a vaccine or a pill can take years. I honestly didn't mean to give you false hope."

He brushed some strands of hair from his mouth. "But what you're saying is, it could mean something in the future...maybe. Right?"

"Maybe," she offered, but the word was measured with caution. "But it could take years of testing before we know for sure. Can you live with that?"

Kash nodded. Hearing it out loud still jarred him. "I can. I think. I don't really have a choice, do I?"

Pressing a gloved hand to his chest, making his stomach do all sorts of weird things in response, Scotty said, "For now, no. You don't. I really would be Dr. Frankenstein if I gave you a transfusion of my blood when you don't need it."

Kash moved his face closer to hers, unable to deny the havoc she was wreaking on his senses. "But you said you'd rather be called Madame Curie. Didn't she research radioactivity? I bet she did lots of things one probably shouldn't do, but look at the end result," he teased.

"She won a Nobel Prize. I get the feeling I'm not in line for one of those—especially because three quarters of the population doesn't know people like you exist. But do note, I'm very impressed you know about her."

"Told you I knew science stuff," he said with a smug smile, fascinated by her lips. "And Miss Marie won not one but *two* Nobel Prizes."

"Dreamy sigh. That you know that is insanely sexy."

"Really?" Kash asked, leaning in closer still, until their lips almost touched. The heart he wasn't sure he still had began to thump in his chest in erratic beats.

"Really," she whispered, seconds before the world around them melted away and Kash pressed his lips to hers.

An explosion of colors flashed behind his eyes when their mouths met. Her lips were soft, gentle, tentative at first, until he couldn't stop himself from deepening their kiss.

Her arms wound around his neck and she stood on tiptoe, letting her body sink into his.

When their tongues met, Kash was sure he'd teeter if not for the tree holding them up. Splaying his hand across her back, he hauled Scotty closer, forgetting how much smaller she was than him. Forgetting everything but the way Scotty felt. She tasted of the wine they'd had with dinner, fruity and rich, and he couldn't get enough.

He couldn't get enough of her soft moan, the way she fit against him like she'd always been there. Everything simply clicked into place.

He'd never experienced the kind of electric rush of waves he currently felt coursing through his limbs by the mere touch of someone's lips.

If Kash was still a breathing kind of guy, and he wasn't sure he was, he'd have stopped by now. Everything he'd ever felt when experiencing desire for another woman paled in comparison to this magnified intensity.

"Uh...guys?"

They pulled apart like they'd been caught in a drug

bust. Kash almost tripped over poor Janet, who'd sat patiently at his feet while he sucked face with the pretty doctor.

Scotty wobbled, but Kash grabbed her by the arm and righted her. They both glanced at Darnell, and by the looks of it, they shared the same guilty expressions.

"We were just..." Scotty started out with a breathless explanation, but swallowed hard, clamping her mouth shut when she must have realized she sounded overwhelmed.

"We were just checking each other's tonsils," he joked. Scotty nudged him hard in the ribs, making him cough. "Uhh. What's up?"

Darnell clearly fought a grin. "Nina texted and said Miss Scotty's got a visitor."

Scotty, who'd been looking down at her feet, obviously to avoid Darnell's eyes, stood up straight. "I've got a visitor? *Me*?"

"Yep." He held up the phone and squinted. "Says his name is Glen. Glen Benson."

Kash cocked his head and looked down at Scotty. "Who's Glen Benson?"

She sighed, and it was a sigh filled with emotions he didn't understand, but he was sure one of them was hesitation.

"My ex-fiancé."

Oh.

SIXTEEN

W hy, why, *why* now? Why would Glen be looking for her now? They hadn't spoken to each other in almost a year, since they'd broken up.

What, in all the whats in the world, would make him come to Buffalo? And how the hell did he find her in the first place?

"Marty says he's at the lab," Darnell provided.

"Thanks, Darnell." And that was all she said. She was still reeling from the single-best kiss she'd ever had in her entire life, so words were at a minimum anyway.

But leave it to Glen to ruin a perfect moment.

Crap. She'd kissed Kash. Oh, Lord. This was not good. It was a mistake. Now what was she going to do? How was she ever going to look him in the eye again?

How was she ever going to forget how his hard

body felt under her fingertips? How delicious his lips were? How he'd evoked visuals of all sorts of naughty images in her head? How she'd never been kissed so voraciously, so thoroughly, *ever*.

Warring with a million questions zipping through her head, Scotty began to head back toward the lab, bowing her head to the wind, her feet suddenly frozen, her hands like icicles.

When she heard Kash following, she stopped and held up a hand. "You don't have to come."

God. She really didn't want him to meet Glen. Not after that kiss. Not ever, despite the kiss. Glen was the biggest embarrassment she'd ever suffered.

Kash's face went bland under the moonlight. "I don't mind."

"I'm def comin'," Darnell said. "Nobody goes anywhere without one of us. We already agreed. So let's git. Doc looks cold." He crossed his beefy arms over his chest and waited for them to move.

They both trudged toward the lab, neither of them saying anything, but Scotty was more worried about why Glen had shown up. She'd have to deal with the kiss later.

At Bobby-Sue, Kash pushed open the door to the lab and motioned for her to go first. As she stepped inside, the glare of the overhead fluorescent lights hurt her eyes. The damp smell of water, however, appeared to be receding.

Glen was there, waiting in the chair Nina had been

sitting in earlier. Tall, handsome, very blond, very spray-tanned, his teeth insanely white, his sport coat and matching trousers pristine.

He'd always hated how pale vampire skin was, so he regularly spray-tanned it away. She'd once admired his good looks. Now, with clearer eyes, he just looked orange.

"Scotty!" he greeted her with a warm smile, opening his arms to embrace her as if he hadn't broken up with her when he'd learned her disease had progressed and things, medically speaking, were only going to get tougher for her.

"Glen." Scotty let him hug her, keeping her butt out, of course. She gave him a quick pat on the back and moved away from him as quickly as her frozen feet allowed. "How did you get in here?"

"A very angry, but stunning vampire named Nina let me in and told me to wait for you."

She was going to have to talk to Nina, for sure. She wasn't sure what to say, so she didn't say anything else.

Despite her lukewarm hug, Glen stayed close to her. "I'm good. How are you?"

She didn't ask him how he was. Wasn't it just like Glen to assume she cared?

Already cranky about allowing Kash to kiss her—about participating so eagerly—she most definitely wasn't in the mood to play nice with Glen for show.

He'd broken up with her in the hospital when she

was sick as a dog, after she'd all but nursed his vampire ass back to health upon discovering he had a rare allergy to a particular type of blood he'd consumed, causing his fangs to rapidly decay and making it impossible for him to feed properly.

She'd made that discovery. She was the one who'd identified his rare, deadly allergy. Just her and her "little microscope" as he'd once called it. No one else had been able to figure it out.

She'd fallen hard for Glen and his charismatic ways, his fake- humble-but-fighting-spirit brag. He was also the primary reason she fought so hard to stay as far from Kash as she could. She'd become too involved with Glen, a one-time patient.

And now look.

She'd all but sucked Kash's lips right off his daggone face.

But every boyfriend she'd had until Glen had done the same thing. They'd left when the going got tough. Why she'd thought Glen would be any different was a mystery.

She was in a lull in her disease right now. But that would change. It always did, and if she allowed herself to become involved with Kash, and things got rough, he'd do the same thing everyone else had.

Leave.

She simply wasn't up to that kind of heartbreak again. Her health had to remain her primary focus.

That and getting Kash back on his feet so he could live his life.

Scotty forgot where she was for a moment until Glen said, "Scotty, Sweet Pea? How ya been?"

Sweet Pea. He'd always called her Sweet Pea. Ugh. Hearing it now infuriated her.

Without hesitation, and maybe because she was still so angry about how they'd broken up, she didn't mince words. "Why are you here, Glen, and how did you find me?"

He put his best hurt face on and made pouty lips. An expression that had once made her legs buttery but now only made her want to punch him in his egotistical noggin.

Glen cocked his head, as though confused at her reception. "I had business in the area and your dad mentioned you were here in Buffalo, too. So he texted me the address and here I am," he said, as though he was some sort of gift. "I thought it'd be fun to surprise you."

All the fun.

Leave it to Banner McNealy to rat her out. He loved Glen. He'd been thrilled when Glen had proposed, and as brokenhearted as she'd been when he'd ended their relationship with a *phone call.*

She suspected most of her father's grief had been due to the fact that she and Glen were from the same clan. Getting married meant she'd have access to some doors her father hadn't had any success opening.

And because they both worked in the same field of finance, they ran into each other from time to time at various conventions and, of course, clan gatherings. Her father, much like Glen, was always looking for a new investment opportunity.

Tightening her jacket around her neck, she shrugged as indifferently as possible. "I'm sort of in the middle of a project, but it was nice seeing you again."

Kash stepped forward then, his tail bobbing, his fin flapping, and the partial wing protrusion poking out of his back, pushing against his jacket.

And even though he looked absolutely hilarious with things poking out of everywhere on his body, he somehow managed to look more like a confident man than Glen ever had.

He stuck out his hand at Glen, his jaw tight. "Kash Samuels."

Glen took Kash's hand with a raised eyebrow and gave it a shake before letting go. "Glen Benson." Then he looked at Scotty with a hitch of his chiseled jaw and an amused glance. "Is *this* your project?"

She didn't like the way he assessed Kash with a smug stare under the harsh glare of the basement lighting. How quickly he'd forgotten what he'd looked like with two holes in his mouth where his fangs should have been and how stupid he'd looked as they grew back.

Kash didn't appear to appreciate how Glen was

evaluating him, either. He puffed his chest out and lifted his chin. He was easily five inches taller than Glen, and certainly outweighed him by a good thirty pounds, and even with all his afflictions, he came across as intimidating.

Darnell instantly stepped in, offering his hand, too. "Darnell the Demon," he said, keeping a smile on his face, but his nostrils twitched.

"*The* Darnell? As in the OOPS Darnell?" Glen asked with awe in his voice. "I've heard so much about you. Such a pleasure to meet you."

Darnell eyed him. The usually cheerful demon had suddenly become wary. "Hadn't heard nuthin' 'bout you. But nice to meet ya just the same."

Scotty fought a giggle before she got serious. "Anyway, it was good seeing you, Glen, but I have some work to finish up, if you don't mind."

Glen shot her his million-dollar smile. "A girl's gotta eat though, right? How about we have dinner together?"

"A girl already ate," Kash said from stiff lips.

But Scotty stepped between the two men, both very clearly posturing. "He's right. A girl did. I'm still stuffed."

"Then maybe a quick drink at my hotel? Whaddya say, Sweet Pea? Promise to have you back in an hour —tops."

"I can't, Glen. I have too much to do. But thanks for stopping by. Take care." With that, head held high, she pushed past him and headed toward the damp lab, where she'd hide until he was gone.

And she hoped that would be soon.

How dare that son-of-a-bitch just show up out of the blue and expect everything to be sweetness and light after he'd left her with the taste of his road dust in her mouth?

Jerk.

And oh boy, her father was going to get a call from her. A big, angry call maybe with some swear words thrown in. He was supposed to protect her, not hope Glen would weasel his way back in so Banner could make connections.

Clenching her fists together, Scotty stuffed one in her mouth to keep from screaming.

"Hey!" Glen said, catching up and grabbing her by the arm, thwarting her movement. "I came all this way to see you. You could at least have a drink with me."

Anger sizzled along her spine as Scotty turned to face him to give him the hell he so richly deserved, but that never happened.

Instead, Kash put a hand on Glen's shoulder, his eyes on fire, his jaw tight. "She said she has work to do. I think it's time you went back to your hotel."

Half of Scotty was angry. She could take care of herself. Sure, because of her disease, she was on the small-ish side and weaker than most, but her voice was plenty strong.

The other half of her appreciated the support.

Still, she held up a hand. "Kash. I've got this, thanks." Turning to Glen, Scotty glared into his very blue eyes. "Glen. I said no. I don't want to have a drink with you. Not now. Not ever. I didn't ask you to come 'all this way' to see me because I didn't want to see you at all. Had I known you were in town, I *still* wouldn't have wanted to see you. Now, please *go*."

Glen lifted his chin and narrowed his eyes, his feet shifting position. "I see. You're still angry about how we left things." He held his hands up in surrender. "I get it. You don't want to be friends."

Friends? Did friends leave you when you were in your darkest hour?

His words incited her, and even though she knew she was giving him what he wanted, she couldn't help herself. "Left things? *We* didn't leave things. *You* left things like the coward you are. So, no. I absolutely don't want to be friends."

His lips—lips she'd once thought were perfect— thinned into an ugly slash across his handsome face. "That's fine. I guess when my family asks how you are, I'll have to tell them we aren't *friends*."

Poor Glen. When he didn't get what he wanted, he reminded people of his clan standing, which happened to be a much higher ranking than her family. Funny how she hadn't realized that until they'd broken up.

The subtle mention of his family and the kind of power they wielded in their clan was just more proof he was a jerk, and it sent her right over the edge.

187

Her father was going to be pretty tweaked, but Scotty decided she didn't care anymore.

She threw up both her middle fingers. "Go to hell, Glen. Now get the fuck out of my lab."

Glen turned his back on her, but before he did, he sneered in a whisper he probably thought only Scotty could hear, unaware Kash's hearing was pretty sharp, "I always knew you could be a bitch—"

That was the last word he said before Kash punched him square in the nose, sending his head and his perfect hair flying.

Then the situation got hairy.

Literally.

CHAPTER

SEVENTEEN

"Kash! Stop it, man!" Darnell yelled in his ear as he tried to yank him off Glen.

Frankly, Scotty was surprised Glen hadn't bitten Kash in defense by now. Maybe he was still having trouble with his fangs?

Kash, on the other hand, was a snarling, drooling, half-shifted raging bull, holding Glen by the throat with one hand and using his bear paw to pummel his face.

He'd knocked the chair Glen had been sitting on clear down the hallway, and the water-damaged treadmill lie on its side after his mad dash to reach him.

"Kash!" She yelled at him so loud, it made her hack a cough. "Kash! Stop!" She grabbed him by the arm just as Darnell successfully pulled his fingers from

Glen's throat, leaving her ex lying on the floor, stunned.

Her breathing became labored from all the excitement, making it hard to focus, as Kash still struggled in Darnell's grip. She had to calm him down or he could begin to seize, and she didn't want that.

"Kash!" She coughed again, praying a spasm wasn't on its way. "Listen to me! Calm down. Please. You're going to seize again if you don't stop. You have to stop!" She'd tranq him if she had to. It was dangerous for him to get so worked up without fully shifting.

"Man, you betta cool it or I'm gonna slug you! I don't wanna, but I will." Darnell warned with a hiss in Kash's ear. "Concentrate, buddy!"

Little by little, Kash appeared to become aware of his surroundings, much the way he had when the water tank broke.

Only this time, he had actually partially shifted into a were. His teeth had elongated, his hair had become scruffy, his nose an almost muzzle. Claws sprang from his fingers and his feet had burst out of his work boots, leaving the leather torn and ragged.

The event was amazing to see, but dangerous to his health.

As Kash heaved rasping breaths, Glen rose from the floor, pressing his wrist to his split lip, his face a bloody mess of scratches and bruises. "What kind of *project* is this, Scotty? Jesus Christ, he's an animal! A damn *freak*!"

That was all Kash needed to hear before he was struggling to get to Glen again while Darnell, obviously using a gargantuan amount of effort, held him back.

Fighting a coughing spasm, she pointed to the metal door, her eyes narrowed. "Glen, shut up and get out! *Get out!*" she screamed.

Pushing his way past Darnell and a livid Kash, he looked as though he wanted to say something in return, but Kash's enraged snarling made him hustle out the door without saying another word.

"What the hell is going on, Doc?"

Trina? What was Trina doing here so late? She could barely get her to stay until five, let alone eight in the evening.

"Trina! Look out!" Darnell shouted as he almost lost his grip on Kash, who fought like a feral animal to get free of his hold.

Trina scooted inside the door Glen had just exited, flattening herself against the light gray concrete wall until she inched her way over to stand next to Scotty. "What the hell's going on now?" she yelled above Kash's agonized roars.

Grabbing Trina's wrist, Scotty pulled her to her side. "I'll tell you all about it later. Right now, I need you to help me get Kash calmed down. Get a tranquilizer before he seizes!"

She sputtered the name of the drug and Trina immediately fluttered off, her wings flapping madly as she pushed her way into the lab, but it wasn't in enough time to keep Kash from escaping Darnell's grasp.

He was out the basement door in a hot second, screeching a bloodcurdling war cry, probably aimed at Glen.

"I'm on it! Text the girls, *now*! You can't be left alone!" Darnell yelled before taking off after Kash.

Grabbing the toppled chair, Scotty set it upright and sat down, her breathing ragged as she pulled her phone from her back pocket and sent a 9-1-1 to the women.

Shit. Shit. Shit. What a damn mess.

"Scotty, you're bleeding!" Trina returned and knelt down beside her. "Let me get something for it."

She pushed Trina's hands away and tried to stand. "No! I have to go get Kash. We have to get to him before he has another seizure."

"The hell you're going anywhere!" Nina yelled, stomping into the basement. "Christ on a bike! What the fuck is going on over here? We could hear somebody howlin' like they were skinned alive!"

Scotty looked up, the side of her neck on fire. "It's Kash. He's partially shifted. We have to help him!"

They all knew how dangerous that was—how hard that could be on him internally. He had to be sedated.

Nina lifted Scotty's chin. "Jesus and fuck, what the hell happened to your neck, Doc?"

"She must have gotten scratched in the scuffle," Trina offered with a shaky voice, back again with some antiseptic and wipes to clean Scotty's wounds.

"You," Nina said, pointing to Trina, her eyes glittering. "Where the fuck is this tranquilizer?"

Trina held up the syringe, filled with a powerful sedative.

"Stay here with the doc and fix her up, I'll tranq Kash." The vampire flew out the door on feet with wings, leaving only Scotty and Trina.

"Doc, these scratches look pretty bad. Let's go into the lab and I'll fix you right up."

Reluctantly, knowing she couldn't do anything to help until they found Kash, she let Trina lead her toward the lab to get cleaned up. Her feet were stiff and her chest was on fire. She coughed yet again, already on her way to a spasm.

Trina asked, "Where's your inhaler, Doc? Take a puff and if that doesn't help, I'll get the nebulizer and we'll do a treatment."

Scotty dug around in the pocket of her jeans and pulled out her inhaler, taking a pull before she sat down on the edge of her ruined desk.

"Lift your chin up and let me clean this. The scratches are kinda deep, but it doesn't look like you need stitches."

Scotty found herself a little impressed when Trina

pulled a compact from her purse and let her see her neck. She was right. They were only surface scratches, but they were ugly and crimson red.

"Someone paid attention in class," she complimented Trina.

Trina just rolled her eyes. "I did manage to make it past first aid-class, but I didn't like it."

Scotty found herself coughing a laugh despite the situation and how much the antiseptic stung. Trina stepping up to the plate caught her off guard, but in a nice way.

The fairy winced as she gently wiped antiseptic-soaked cotton balls over her neck, simultaneously handing Scotty her portable nebulizer. She took deep breaths of the warm medicine, allowing it to loosen the tightness of her lungs.

When she was done, Trina asked, "So what in all of hell happened out there? How did the scratches happen?"

Scotty really had to think about that as she inhaled. "To be honest, I don't have a clue. Kash was attacking Glen, and like you said, I must have been caught up in it somehow. I don't even remember feeling it happen."

"Well, it's a doozy. He's really cute and all, but I'm not sure it makes up for how violent this turn has made him. Do you really think you can help fix this?"

She was determined to help him. Kash couldn't live his life like this, with his body at constant war with his emotions. "I'm going to find a way to get him to fully shift into something—*anything*. I'm convinced that'll help."

The old Trina returned, sullen and moody. "If you say so."

She didn't have time to argue in defense of her research skills, but she was curious about something. "Hey, why are you here so late? I thought you'd be long gone by now after everything that happened today. It's almost eight-thirty. No hip bars open tonight?"

Trina made a face at her. "Oh, trust and believe. I was long gone, but I forgot something so I came back."

Scotty was too busy scrolling her phone for a message from Nina or one of the others to ask what she'd forgotten. She'd just be grateful Trina had been around to help.

Her phone pinged an incoming message, making her hop off the desk. "They found him!" Noting her voice sounded far more excited than she'd like, Scotty cleared her throat and squared her shoulders. "Thanks for your help, Trina. I'd better go and check on Kash now. Will you lock up?"

"Yep. See you tomorrow." She saluted her and turned back around to gather her purse.

Scotty coughed out another thank you to Trina and left the lab, her ribs already starting to ache from coughing so hard.

"There you are!" Marty called with a smile. "I'm on official Doc duty." She offered Scotty her arm, leading her back to the guesthouse. As they walked, Marty placed her arm around her shoulders and pulled her in. "You don't sound good. I could hear you coughing all the way back at the guesthouse and your breathing is rattling."

"That's your exceptional hearing at play. I'm better now. I had a nebulizer treatment and it's eased the coughing."

Marty squeezed Scotty's shoulders. "Still, you're worrying us, Scotty. You, maybe even more than Kash, have to watch your health. *Nothing* comes before that."

"This has happened so often in my life, it's just another chapter in my disease."

Marty stopped then and looked at Scotty, her eyes warm and oh so blue. "You know, I don't even know what you have. Does it have a name?"

"It's a rare genetic disease called Kabalo syndrome. It affects my organs, my growth, weakens my muscles. It's degenerative. It's why I'm so small, despite how much I eat."

Snowflakes fell in Marty's eyelashes and on her cheeks. "Wait..." Her voice hitched. "Does that mean... does that mean you'll..."

She filled in the blank without hesitation. "Die. Yep. The longest recorded life for someone who lived with Kabalo was thirty-seven."

Marty bit her lips, her eyes wet with unshed tears. "And you're thirty...?"

"Seven."

Marty swallowed, squeezing her shoulders, her lower lip trembling. "I knew you were sick, but I didn't know you were this sick, Scotty. What can we do to help?"

"Listen, I take solace in the fact that it's now been two hundred and eighty-two days since I surpassed the last-known recorded death from this disease. So there's that. There's nothing you can do to help, but I'm hoping the research I've been doing will amount to something soon."

"Are you close?" she asked as the snow fell around them and her sorrow filled the air.

Scotty shook her head. "No. Not as close as I'd like. I thought Kash's change might help—in terms of how unusual it is—but I think we saw how that worked out."

Marty blew out a breath. "Yeah. Your blood turned his human, but his did nothing to yours." She pulled Scotty in for a hug and whispered against the top of her head. "Listen, I didn't know it was this serious—or maybe imminent is the word I'm looking for. Nina told us you were sick, but I think we all thought that diagnosis was a long way off. God, I feel like such a ninny."

"Don't. Death is a difficult subject. I'm used to it."

Marty looked at her long and hard, as though she were trying to get into her head and fish around. But then she asked, "I guess you haven't told Kash?"

She kept her answer light. "Why would I? He's my patient. I'm his doctor. There's nothing to tell him."

Marty's eyes gazed deeply into hers. "I think we both know that's not true. You like him. He likes you. There's nothing wrong with that, Scotty. In fact, it's a little wonderful to find someone you like, someone you have undeniable chemistry with."

And someone whose kiss is unmatched by another.

"But it's not so wonderful if you're dying, is it?" she asked, keeping her eyes on the snow-covered ground, fighting the onslaught of tears.

Marty swallowed hard again but she didn't say a word. Instead, she wrapped her in a warm hug.

Scotty accepted Marty's vanilla-and-pear-scented embrace, closing her eyes and reveling in the comfort. It felt like a long time since someone had hugged her.

But then she straightened and smiled at Marty, pulling away from her embrace. "And anyway, it might still be."

"What might still be?"

"A long-way-off diagnosis. I've made it this far, right? I mean, I already beat that guy's record, right? Who knows. I might make it to thirty-eight yet."

Marty chucked her under the chin and gave her a watery smile. "Not if we don't get you inside. So c'mon. Let's get you warm."

Scotty let Marty lead her to the porch of the guest-house, but before they went in, she stopped her short and squeezed her hand, pressing it to her cold cheek. "You're one badass, Scotty McNealy."

Scotty looked at her for a moment, absorbing her praise, wanting to remember how beautiful this new friend of hers was. "That says a lot coming from someone like you."

She gave Marty another hard hug before going inside to see what Kash was facing now. But she'd always remember this moment due to its rarity in her life.

No one had ever called her a badass before.

But it was kinda nice.

EIGHTEEN

S cotty stared down at Kash, sleeping so peacefully after being jabbed with a sedative by Nina, and all she wanted to do was brush his silky pink strands of hair away from his face.

He'd mostly morphed back into the Kash they'd all come to know with the exception of the hair on his face, but he looked worn down.

There were dark shadows under his eyes and creases in his forehead she hadn't noticed before—and believe, she'd seen him up close enough to know they hadn't existed before tonight.

His arms were pretty scratched up from running willy-nilly through the woods. She'd treated them with an antiseptic and wrapped them, otherwise he was mostly fine.

So fine.

Her cheeks went suddenly hot when she remembered that kiss.

"He sleeping?" the vampire asked, approaching the bed. "Or do you need me to knock the shit out of him again?"

Scotty fought laughter. "No. No beating him up. He'll beat himself up enough when he realizes he clocked Glen."

"No the hell he won't," Kash muttered sleepily. "I don't feel a shred of guilt for popping that guy in his perfect face. He called you a rude name. Feminism be damned, that'll never fly with me."

Nina nodded her agreement, plopping down on the bed next to Kash's feet and flicking his toes with her fingers. "Kinda gotta roll with Burgermeister on this. If the asshole was calling you names, I'd have punched him, too."

She planted her hands on her hips, looking down at his bulky frame covered in Marty's comforter. "That you punched him isn't the point, and you know it. You reacted violently, Kash. There was no getting you away from him once you had him in your grip. That has to be controlled. It's time we work harder on getting you to focus on shifting into at least one thing—*fully*. We need to flesh out your abilities and make them stronger, not cater to everything at once. I think that's been our mistake."

Kash pushed his way to a sitting position, the muscles in his arms rippling. "I don't totally get what you mean, but okay. The guy was still a dick and it wouldn't matter who you were, or what I was, I still wouldn't let him talk to anyone that way. Male or female."

She ignored the bit about Glen. She didn't want to talk about him. "I mean, seeing as werewolf appears to be the most predominant paranormal trait you possess, the one that shows up to the party first, let's focus all our energy on that."

"But what happens to everything else? Like my fin? My bear paw? I think I've grown attached," he joked.

She'd given this some serious thought and talked it over with a fellow colleague—one who she knew would keep his mouth shut—via Skype while Kash had slept off the sedation. "The new course of action is to behave as though they don't exist. But only until we can get you fully shifted. If you still have a fin and a bear paw once you've made the transition, we'll focus on those next. We just need to nail one thing first."

Kash was silent for a moment, but when he spoke, his voice was filled with remorse. "I tore stuff up again, didn't I?"

Nina snorted. "There wasn't much left in the lab to tear up except for that asshole. You tore him up but good, dude. Darnell said he looked like ground beef when you were done. And he's a vampire—so kudos. Also, you've gotten a fuckload faster. Shit, you almost outran me. But I got you, motherfucker. Had to tackle your ass to do it, but I gotcha."

Kash looked as though he was trying to keep his

face impassive, but it was impossible for him not to hide his obvious pride in outrunning the master.

Then, all at once, he went contrite when he looked at Scotty—and finally noticed her neck. "Jesus Christ. Please tell me I didn't do that to your neck?"

Scotty's hand fluttered under her chin. "It's fine. It's just some superficial scratches."

But Kash shook his head, his expression one of misery. "No, Scotty. I hurt you. *Jesus*. Please know I would never hurt you on purpose." He held out his hand, but she pretended to ignore it.

"You *didn't* do it on purpose, Kash. It was an accident. I just got caught up in the melee."

"I'm so sorry. I behaved poorly, and it was wrong. It seems when I get angry, I see red. But I'm going to try as hard as I can to get this under control."

His fight with Glen to protect her, and her conversation with Marty about how she'd surpassed the last Kabalo syndrome death date, reminded her why she couldn't get involved. Not just with Kash, but with anyone.

She knew there were good men out there. Obviously the OOPS ladies had three husbands who were all ride or die, but her fear of being hurt again, of being as devastated as she'd been when Glen broke up with her, and the fact that she was going to die of this disease, kept her rooted in absolute terror.

Kash would likely live forever, much like all paranormals, but she might not even be able to promise him a full year. Who wanted to start a relationship with that on their plate? She didn't. She wouldn't.

Maybe she was jumping the gun and a kiss was just a kiss to him. Maybe it was no big deal and she was turning it into something it wasn't.

Nina stood up then and stretched her arms over her head with a yawn. "You're killin' me with all your flights of fancy. Knock that shit off, huh? I'm gonna go down and read with Carl before he goes to bed. Stop turning into the Incredible Hulk and let us chill for at least one night."

Kash chuckled then winced, putting a hand over his stomach. "You bet. Tell Carl I said good night."

"I'll send Janet to you in a little bit. I have a bone with her name on it." Nina waved and left the bedroom, leaving them and only the sound of awkward silence.

"Boy, Janet's gonna hate going home. She's never been so spoiled." When she didn't respond, he said, "Scotty?"

She looked down at her feet, now encased in thick, warm socks. "Uh-huh?"

"C'mere. Sit next to me. Let's talk."

Oh, no. No, no, nope-ity-nope. No more Mr. Magic Lips. Taking a step back, she shook her head as if confused. "About?"

"About what happened when we were walking Janet, and with Glen, too. Everything."

Licking her dry lips, because she wasn't very good

at this and she was usually the one broken up with, she put on a serious face and looked him in the eye.

Which was more than she could say for Glen. He'd broken up with her over the phone. The dick.

She put her hands behind her back, clasping them together. "Listen, Kash. This isn't a good idea. I mean, it was just a kiss, and the thing with Glen, well, he was being a dick. I get why he triggered you, and we're going to learn how to control that if it's the last thing I do."

There. Were they broken up yet? Not that they were a couple, but she was drawing a line in the sand using her words like an adult. Even if the words cut her to the core, cut her in a way she couldn't explain. Surely, she shouldn't feel this devastated over something that had barely happened.

But that kiss...

Kash sat up straighter, straightening his shredded sweater. "Just a kiss? *Just a kiss?*"

Scotty stared at him dumbly, feigning innocence. "That's what I said. It was just a kiss."

He scowled with a scoff. "You know that's not true, Scotty. I know you felt what I felt, and you're lying if you say you didn't. Chalk it up to my new senses, but I could smell it on you. We had a moment, Scotty. Don't tarnish it by saying we didn't."

She rolled her eyes the way she did at her father. She had loads of practice at it. "And it was a nice moment. But that's all it was. I have a career I'm committed to right now, Kash. I don't want any other commitments, and patients and doctors hooking up is always a bad idea anyway. We have lots of work to do so we can get you back to your life. Let's just leave it at that, okay?"

Clearly, he was stunned to silence, and that was for the best.

"Get some sleep, Kash. Tomorrow's a big day." Turning on her heel, she hoped to make a graceful exit.

Unfortunately, she tripped on the area rug and almost fell.

Which felt par for the course on today of all days.

DARNELL SMILED at him with two thumbs up. "Okay, you got the image in your head, Kash?"

"Think about Kash in werewolf form, a handsome creature of the night, preparing to roam the frozen woods with grace and majesty, uninhibited by man's mortal trappings," Marty encouraged.

"Wow, Boss," Darnell praised. "Nice visual. Almost turned me into one'a you."

She curtsied with a grin, holding out her skirt when she did. "Thank you. Now visualize, Kash."

And he did—or at least he tried, yet, he couldn't concentrate on much else but Scotty and the rejection she'd lobbed in his face almost a week ago.

Since then, she'd been all business. Taking blood at

regular intervals, running all sorts of tests, and basi-cally acting as though he didn't exist as anything but a means to an end.

And dammit all, it kinda hurt his feelings. They had indeed had a moment. She couldn't deny it, because a new part of him, one he'd never been aware of before, said so.

Marty and the girls all said his instincts would become sharper with each day that passed, and if that was the case, where Scotty was concerned, they were sharp as a knife.

Because every day, he literally felt the rhythm of her body without ever touching her. He smelled her moods—which were mostly dour unless she was with Janet or Espy. He smelled something else, too. Worry, maybe? He couldn't be sure.

Still, he'd promised himself he'd do as Scotty asked —because when a lady said no, that meant no. He didn't like it. He'd change it if she'd let him, but he'd done everything he could to keep himself in line. He'd avoided her in the hall of the guesthouse, in the kitchen when they got too close, in the lab when she put her fingers around his wrist to take his pulse.

He wanted all the things she didn't, and no matter how mind-blowing their kiss had been, they saw two very different futures for themselves.

"Hey, did you guys ever hear from the Skinwalker Association?" he asked, trying to focus on something other than Scotty sitting in the corner, working on her computer, wearing a red turtleneck that hugged her figure in all the right places.

He was getting pretty good at sneaking glances at her when she wasn't looking, like some lame kid with a crush.

They'd had a near collision in the hallway the other day, but he'd managed to wind his tail around his neck—a tail that had suddenly become quite sensitive—and scoot around her, never meeting her eyes.

Marty's laughter tinkled through the reconstructed lab. "There's no association of skinwalkers, silly man. There are only a couple of them that we know of, and they appear to be decidedly unreachable. Go figure, right? Anyway, in essence, nope. No new information. Now quit talking and start visualizing."

"I can't help you with the werewolf part, but I can help you with your unruly emotions," Wanda said, folding her hands together in front of her. "While you're visualizing your majesty and grace, think of something that calms you. What relaxes you, Kash? For me, it's my husband and my children. I think of home when I'm feeling vexed and I want to use my vampire skills for bad."

Wanda's mention of her children and husband made him feel like shit. The women were all here, trying like hell to help him, and their families suffered for it. Though they took breaks and went home for a few hours each day, they were never very far from him.

Home.

That felt very far away right now, but he definitely missed the comfort of enjoying a good shot of whiskey in a hot cup of coffee while sitting on his back porch— even bundled up in a coat due to the crappy weather. That always made him happy.

Suddenly, a loud rash of gasps went through the room, pulling him from his thoughts.

He looked at everyone, his head cocked. "What? What's wrong now?"

Scotty had stopped doing whatever she'd been doing on her computer, her jaw unhinged.

He all but stamped his feet when he demanded, "*What, guys?*"

Scotty picked up the hand mirror she had on her desk, so he could see his shift if it happened, and walked toward him holding it up.

He didn't need her to get very close. He probably could have seen his image from a hundred miles away, but he loved how she smelled, so he'd take what he could get.

Kash didn't think he had any surprise or shock left in him.

Except he did.

And seeing the waterfall of bright pink hair cascading over his shoulders, the fact that his clothes had all fallen away, and he was now covered in scales, definitely shocked him.

It shocked the *shit* out of him.

Yes, indeed.

CHAPTER
NINETEEN

"Whoa," was the only word Scotty could utter. "Whoa, whoa, whoa."

They all stood around, Trina included, everyone rooted in place until Nina came bounding through the door with Carl in tow, walking right past Kash before she also put the brakes on and stopped, her eyes flying wide open.

She sniffed him up and down with a smug grin on her face before taking a step back, her hands on her hips. "Should we call Esther and Fish Sticks and ask them if they know a good fucking hairdresser?"

Scotty's throat went dry. They'd been talking werewolves last she'd checked while she pretended to be busy with super-important test results that didn't exist so she could methodically ignore Kash's presence.

"Who are Esther and Fish Sticks?" Scotty croaked, biting her lip with a wince.

"Esther's a fucking mermaid and Fish Sticks…er, Tucker, is her mate. They're mermaids or mermen or what the fuck ever. They're big fish, for shit's sake. Esther was a case we worked on a couple years ago. Now she's off making baby fish sticks."

How had they gotten here? How had Kash visualized *this*?

She approached him with care. Kash was sexy as hell, but as a merman, he had a powerful seductive quality, a crazy manliness about him with his broad, rippled-with-muscle chest exposed.

His scales glistened under the fluorescent lighting of the lab, green and lavender, soft, muted colors that changed when the light hit them. And his hair?

As if every girl on planet Earth who liked long hair wouldn't love to have his pink locks. They were silky, shiny-soft with just the right amount of bounce, cascading down around his wide shoulders to just past his waist.

She'd done everything possible to stay out of his way, and he'd honored her request, as well, making the temptation of him simply breathing drive her almost out of her mind for the last week.

Not to mention, she felt really strange. This particular phase of her disease wasn't mentioned anywhere, in all of her years of research. But there were moments in the past several days when she felt amazing. When the world around her became a thing of wonder.

She wanted to touch everything, feel the texture of a knobby pillow, savor the soft fur on Espy's back. Study the fresh flowers Marty had brought home one night to put on the dinner table and inhale their scent.

And then there were moments in her days when it all went to hell. Moments when the simple effort of reaching across her body to grab the remote on her nightstand for the TV in her room felt as monumental as pushing a boulder uphill.

Moments when she didn't care about anything because she was, after all, dying. It kind of made the point of living moot.

As a scientist and doctor, she knew that almost any medical situation had phases. For instance, women on the brink of motherhood nested.

Some patients in the end stages of a disease reported what was loosely and unofficially referred to as terminal lucidity, wherein they appeared much better, more alert and filled with energy. It was very common in Alzheimer's patients. Often, they experienced an unexpected clear mental state.

But there'd never been any reports about Kabalo having any of those symptoms. Of course, the disease was so rare only one in ten million people had it.

Whatever this was plaguing her, she wasn't coughing or out of breath, and that was a blessing. She hadn't needed her inhaler in over three days—a miracle in her world.

But the stranger she felt, the more certain she was that she'd done the right thing by telling Kash they couldn't take their relationship any further.

If only she could convince her heart that her mind had made the right choice, maybe it wouldn't beat so hard when he was around.

Or when he looked like a damn water god.

"Kash?" Wanda called his name, her eyes wary, her expression hesitant. "Can you tell us what you were thinking about when you were visualizing?"

He blinked, still staring in the mirror. "Um... I was thinking...about my house. Sitting on the...the porch and having some...uh, coffee. With a splash of whiskey."

Marty sighed and chastised him. "Is that at all majestic, Kash Samuels? I told you to think about roaming through the woods. It's the were in you we have to get under control, not the merman."

"I'm sorry. It just happened when Wanda mentioned her kids and husband. It made me think about how shitty I feel for keeping you guys from your families, and that got me thinking about my house, and now...this." He spread his arms wide to indicate his latest form.

"But!" Darnell declared with a wide smile. "You visualized and you shifted into a whole merman, dude! Gimme a knuck!" He held out his fist for Kash to bump.

Kash held out his fist but didn't look at Darnell, he was too fascinated by the shape his body had taken.

Nina leaned toward Scotty, giving her a nudge with her shoulder. "Didja notice he fucking shifted all the way, Doc? No sign of were. Maybe he's meant to be a merman and not an ass-sniffer?"

"Hmm," she murmured, completely perplexed. "Maybe."

But then Kash's final fin appeared—his tail fin—eliminating his feet altogether—and he fell to the floor with a crash, flopping about like a literal fish out of water.

"Or not," the vampire said on a cackle.

Scotty winced. "I know next to nothing about mermen or their female counterparts. Maybe we should call your friends?"

"On it!" Marty said, pulling her phone from the pocket of her sweater.

"Scotia?"

A chill ran along her spine. No one called her Scotia. Almost never. No one except her father.

She whirled around to find Banner McNealy, tall, lanky, stately in a black suit with a blue pinstriped shirt, sauntering into her lab.

He was an imposing force to almost everyone with his steely blue gaze and sharpish features. Except for, of course, Nina, who was in front of Banner in a millisecond, giving him her menacing eyes and defensive stance.

"Who the fuck's asking?"

Banner blinked in confusion, something Scotty had never seen him do. No one talked to him that way. "You are?"

Scotty wanted to stop Nina and introduce her father, but this was too much fun. He'd told Glen where she was, and after calling to give him hell, she'd had a pin put to her bubble of anger when she discovered he was out of town.

So she'd left him a semi-terse voice mail, which was what had likely prompted this visit.

Nina crossed her arms over her chest, narrowing her dark eyes. "Your worst fucking nightmare if you don't identify yourself."

"Nina!" both Wanda and Marty yelped in an admonishing tone.

Banner's expression indicated horror at Nina's poor manners, so Scotty decided it was time to step in. "Dad, this is Nina Statleon from OOPS. You know, the people you told me not to disappoint?"

Banner cleared his throat, because appearances were always important. Offering Nina his hand, he instantly plastered a smile on his lean face. "Ms. Statleon, it's an honor."

She didn't take his hand, but she did look over her shoulder at Scotty. "So this is Big Daddy Vampire. I thought you'd be fucking scarier."

Her father actually laughed, tucking his hand into the lapel of his suit jacket. "I'll work on that. Until then, I can't tell you what a pleasure it is to meet you all."

Wanda was the first to give Banner a welcoming smile. She held out her ever-so-elegant hand. "Mr. McNealy, I'm Wanda Jefferson. We spoke on the phone."

He took her hand in his and gave it a warm pat. "Of course, you're as lovely as I thought you'd be. So wonderful to meet you."

Marty waved her fingers at Banner and smiled, too, on her way out the door. "Marty Flaherty. Resident werewolf. Nice to meet you, Mr. McNealy."

Trina fluttered her wings and waved, as well. "I'm Trina. You know my dad, Berkley Sutter. Nice to meet you, Mr. McNealy."

Banner blustered, tilting his graying head in that way he had that said he was all atwitter over meeting such superstars. "Please, all of you, call me Banner."

Darnell, who'd helped scoop Kash up off the floor and had him propped up beside him, gave Banner a wink. "Darnell. The demon, in case you wondered. I'd shake your hand but as you can see, I'm kinda busy. Pleasure, sir."

Banner graciously nodded. "Same, son. And this?" He pointed to Kash in all his pink-haired glory. "Is this the reason you were summoned by the esteemed ladies of OOPS?"

Scotty's face flushed with embarrassment. "He's not a *this*, Dad. His name is Kash Samuels, and yes. He's why I'm here—representing and all." Scotty pounded her chest and flashed a sideways peace sign at her father, who frowned in confusion at her gesture.

"Of course. My apologies, Kash. Good to meet you. Sorry for your troubles."

With the aid of Darnell, Kash shook his hand. "Same. Sorry it isn't under less fishy circumstances."

Banner stared at him with an expression that said his gaze was as dead as his sense of humor. Scotty laughed and gave her father a nudge in the ribs. "He's joking, Dad."

Her father visibly relaxed and gave Kash a weak smile. "Glad you still have your sense of humor. Might I steal my daughter from her very important work? I won't take up much of your time."

Marty came rushing back in then, a thick green garden hose with a sprayer attachment trailing behind her. "Talked to Esther and Fish Sti...um, Tucker, and they said we have to keep him wet until he shifts back or his gills could wither up." She shook the hose at them. "I gotta hose him down. Look out below, guys!" she yelled before pulling the handle and shooting a sputtering gush of water at Kash.

"Hey!" he bellowed, putting his hands up. "That's cold and you're gonna mess up my hair!"

Scotty sighed. The conversation she was about to embark on was better off taking place somewhere else.

"Let's go out in the hall, Dad."

Banner put his hand at her waist and led her outside the lab, where much raucous laughter and Kash's protests prevailed.

Once outside the door, she turned to see her father brushing invisible lint from his suit. "How's Mom?"

"Livia's well, Scotia. Worried about you as always, but well."

She smiled. She loved her mother, who, even though she enjoyed keeping up appearances as much as her father, was the warmer of the two.

"Tell her I'm fine and I'll call her soon."

He cupped her cheek. "You look...different. I can't quite explain it."

Hah! Neither could she.

"But it suits you," he was quick to say. He paused for a moment, then pointed to her neck. "What happened, Scotia?"

"Hazard of the job with you bunch of kooky para-normals. Now, what brings you here? Are you checking to be sure I'm not sullying the good McNealy name?"

Her father sighed a rather long, "over it all" sigh. "Sweetheart, why do you always say things like that?"

"Because it's true. You're always reminding me of who you are in the community and who I'm supposed to be as a result. It's standard practice."

He paused for a moment and looked at her long and hard. Only this time, instead of looking refreshed the way he always did, he looked tired. "Being a

McNealy isn't always easy for me. Especially being a *male* McNealy. There are centuries of burdens that come with it. I'm sorry if I've burdened you, in turn, with the albatross around my neck."

"Try being a female and a *human* McNealy. Then we'll talk."

Banner bowed his head, his thick graying hair perfectly combed. "I know, and I'm sorry, darling. That was never the intent. Never."

Wait. Just hold on right there. Was this Banner McNealy *apologizing*?

No. No way.

Hold the phone. Was he dying?

Leave it to her dad to try and out-unlive her.

TWENTY

"Are you dying, Dad?"

He made a face. "*What*? What kind of absurd thing is that to ask, Scotia?"

"Well, something's definitely wrong. I've never heard you apologize for anything, and especially to me. Is this some kind of mid-century crisis?"

Banner actually laughed, pulling her into an impulsive hug. A. Hug. What was happening?

"No, honey. I just recently realized how much of my childhood I've imposed on you. That's all."

She leaned back in his arms, alarmed. "Just recently? Okay, Dad, seriously. What's going on here?"

"Your mother," he said quite plainly, his tone full of what she thought could be defined as misery.

"Mom? What did she do?"

"She threatened to leave me. We've been married

for almost two hundred and fifty years, Scotia. I'm quite blindsided."

Scotty was rocked to the core. Her mother had threatened to leave her father? "But why, Dad? What the heck happened?"

He looked positively wretched. "She said I'm too rigid and that I suck the fun out of everything. I'm a fun-sucker, were her exact words."

Scotty couldn't help herself—she laughed out loud. It wasn't a lie. Her mother wasn't a barrel of laughs either, but she definitely had a lighter take on things than he did.

Maybe her mother behaved that way because it was expected of her. Maybe she was more gregarious than she'd ever let on, but she kept it in check because of Banner...

"Banner McNealy too rigid? Naw. Say it ain't so!"

His shoulders sagged in defeat. "I don't know what to do, Scotia. But our problems aren't yours. In no way shall I put you in the middle of your mother and I. That's not at all why I'm here. Suffice it to say, we've been in counseling and I've learned a thing or two about not only my relationship with your mother, but with *you*."

Scotty didn't know what to say, so she stepped out of his arms with a cautious response. "What have you learned?"

He ran a finger down her nose and smiled. "That

I'm far too worried about what others will say and not worried enough about how that makes everyone around me feel. Most especially with my daughter. That was made abundantly clear by both your mother and your voice mail, regarding Glen."

Suddenly feeling flush, she leaned against the basement wall, letting the cool concrete seep into her back. "Okay... How so?"

Driving his hands into his trouser pockets, her father tipped his head, his eyes full of regret. "I'm always trying to keep the clan happy. With my performance as a clan member, with my work, with how we appear to the outside world. Glen's father, being an important member of the clan, had me putting him before you, and that should have never happened. Nothing is more important to me than you and your mother, Scotia. *Nothing*. I'm sorry I told Glen you were here."

She grabbed his hand and squeezed . "He got really pushy with me, Dad. What I'm doing here is important, and interference from Glen only made things worse. It felt like you were taking his side in our breakup, and that hurt."

He squeezed her hand back. "So you said in your voice mail, and for that I apologize. *Profoundly*. I'm so proud of you and your work, Scotia. Kash looks like he really needs your help. Poor boy."

She laughed, feeling a bit lighter. "He's definitely in a pickle."

"And you, Scotia? How are you feeling?"

She couldn't remember the last time her father had asked her how she was feeling, but she supposed when someone's dying, that's a loaded question. Her father not being good with emotion probably made it that much harder.

His brow furrowed and suddenly, he was holding her hand tighter. "You're not answering. Have things gotten worse?"

"No, Dad. No. I'm just not used to..."

"Me asking how you are."

She shrugged. Now she was uncomfortable. "Well, yeah. You hardly ever talk about my condition and the fact that I'm...well, that I'm dying."

She never shied away from the truth. She knew what her fate would be and she'd tried like hell to find a way to change it. But more than likely, she wouldn't.

She'd love to talk to her parents about it, but they always clammed up, stoically standing by her with each test result and bad bit of news without ever addressing how they felt.

Scotty always wanted to reassure them it was okay to have feelings about her disease, but they never appeared to be as affected as one would expect.

Banner winced, his voice gravelly and deep when he said, "Because it hurts too much to think about. To know I'll live an eternity without you tortures my very soul, Scotia. From the day you were born and we found out you were human. Before we knew about your disease, we knew we'd outlive you. No parent wants that, darling. So I hid. I pulled the covers over my head and hid. But I realize now that it was selfish not to acknowledge your diagnosis. Your fears about...about dying. I'm so deeply sorry."

Her heart ached. She'd never heard him admit something so big. "Oh, Dad..."

He pulled her close again, resting his chin on top of her head. "I can't bear to even speak it. Rather than address it head on, I've avoided it at all costs, and that was self-centered and selfish, and I'm sorry, honey. I'm so incredibly sorry."

Tears fell down her cheeks as she rested her head on her father's chest. "Well, the good news is, so far everything's okay. I'm feeling all right."

And weird. She felt weird. But she didn't want to tell him that. For now, this was enough.

He gripped her shoulders and held her away from him. "I want to talk in depth about this, if you're agreeable. Once you're done here with Kash. Will you have lunch with me?"

"Wow," she said with a pat to the lapels of his jacket. "Therapy's really knocked you for a loop, huh? I mean, you can't even eat lunch."

But he simply said, "Which makes it even sweeter that I'm buying, yes?"

Scotty chuckled, a heavy weight leaving her chest. "I hope your wallet's ready for this appetite."

He grinned down at her, his lean face much lighter.

"Whatever it takes to make things right. So lunch? Soon?"

"Absolutely," she whispered.

He pulled her back toward him one more time and whispered back, "I love you, Scotia. So very much."

And then he was gone, leaving her overwhelmed by all these new feelings blanketing her soul.

Scotty leaned back against the wall and took deep breaths, feeling light-headed and uncharacteristically melancholy as she wiped tears from her cheeks.

"Hey, Doc, you okay?" Nina asked, poking her head out the door, her eyes penetrating Scotty's, searching.

"I don't know." She paused, closing her eyes and shaking her head. "I mean, yes. But I don't know." Then she laughed at the irony. "I feel like that phrase has become an epidemic around here."

Nina grinned, stepping outside to stand in front of her. "It's pretty fucking popular when shit like this goes down."

"I'll bet. How's Kash doing? Has he shifted back?"

She snorted. "Mostly. He's still got some scales, but his fins are gone and his feet are back."

Her eyebrows lifted in surprise. "Even the one on his ankle?"

"Yeah. It was some crazy shit to watch."

"Video or it didn't happen," she joked.

"Are you fucking kidding me? I got video for days, kiddo."

Scotty rubbed Nina's arms. "It's like you read my

mind, Marshmallow." She pushed off the wall, ready to head back in and deal with whatever came next with Kash, when Nina grabbed her hand.

"Hey. Got a serious question."

Scotty looked into her beautiful eyes, drawn in by how dark her lashes were, how absolutely flawless she was, and how little she cared about that.

Tilting her head, she said, "Sure. I'll try and give you a serious answer. What's up?"

Tucking her hair behind her ears with her free hand, she asked, "You got feelings for Burgermeister?"

"What? No. He's my patient, don't talk crazy." God, that sounded like a thinly weak protest even to her ears.

"You said you'd give me a serious fucking answer. So give it to me, and don't lie. 'Cause I'll know."

Her shoulders sagging, Scotty let go of Nina's hands, driving them into the pockets of her lab coat. "I don't know what you want me to say."

"The fucking truth."

"Okay, yes. *Yes*, I have feelings for him. It's wrong. I know it's wrong, and I've been avoiding him ever since I realized it because he's my patient."

"That fucking Slick Willy Glen was your patient, too, wasn't he?"

Scotty almost gasped. "How did you know?"

"I fished around online. It bugs the shit outta me that I don't know who came after Kash that day, pretending to be me. So I've been fiddling with anyone new who's shown up. I found some old pics of you guys on his Facebook page, from the hospital and at a couple of parties. Put two and two together."

"Yes. He was my patient and then my fiancé."

"And then he shit on you?"

"Took a big ol' dump."

"Burgermeister isn't Slick Willy, Scotty. He's fucking not. I can smell it."

"And?"

She shrugged. "I just wanted you to know. I don't have to read your fucking genius mind to know what's going through it, kiddo. I know what state your health is in. It's breakin' my heart, but I know. And I know that's what's keeping you from Mr. Accidental As Fuck. But I also know he'd take whatever time you have left. He'd be all in."

Her throat grew so tight, she thought it would burst. "But I'm..."

"Yeah. I know. You're dying. But just an observation and then I'll leave it the hell alone. I think you use that as a fucking defense mechanism. It's easy to say you can't enjoy life because you don't have much of it left. It's a fuck of a lot harder to try and do it anyway."

Tears welled in Scotty's eyes. She didn't know what to say or how to react to someone as crusty as Nina speaking with so much sensitive wisdom.

In that moment, Scotty didn't care how much Nina

hated displays of affection. She didn't care if it annoyed her. She threw her arms around the vampire's neck and hugged her as hard as she could, burying her face in the silky scent of her raven hair.

Pressing her cheek to Nina's, she murmured, "I like you way more than you'll ever be comfortable with, and I know that you hate that, but I don't care. I think it might even be a bit of a girl-crush."

"You sure don't hug like somebody who's dyin'." She squeezed Scotty hard then disentangled her long limbs from Scotty's clinging ones. "Now get the hell off me and get back in that lab. We need to figure out how to merge all this fucker's personalities so he can get the fuck outta my face."

She smiled with all the warmth she felt for this woman. "I'm on it."

Pushing her way back into the lab, she found everyone standing very still, staring at her with big, round eyes.

Aw, hell. Now what?

Kash had indeed almost entirely shifted back to his former self, including the fin on his ankle, but he didn't look happy.

"Well, look at you," she crooned, mostly pleased with the end result. "Did you do that with visualization or did it just happen?"

He crossed his arms over his shirtless chest, his lips a thin line, and approached her on bare feet.

She frowned as he got closer, confused by his clear anger. "What's wrong?"

"You wanna tell me when you planned to mention you were dying?"

TWENTY-ONE

"Kash..."

He held up a hand in her direction, his jaw tightening. "Not yet, okay? I don't want to make this about me, because that's wrong and it definitely isn't. I just need to process."

Her chest rose and fell, her heart chugging harder in her chest than it ever had before. "Okay," she whispered, her voice hitching.

Kash pushed past her, stalking out the door shirtless, his partial wing still poking out of his shoulder blade.

When he left, there was a moment of silence before everyone rushed at her at once, enveloping her in a group hug.

Well, except for Trina. A glance at the clock on the wall told her it was two minutes after five. She must have somehow slipped out without Scotty noticing.

She relished the hugs from the group, soaking in their words of encouragement.

"I should have told him from the start." She'd probably always regret that decision for whatever life she had left.

Wanda cupped her chin, her eyes shiny with sympathy. "The truth is always best, but we all get why you didn't tell him, and he will, too. Just give him a sec to get his head around this. He knew something was wrong, he just didn't know how wrong, honey. Let him absorb."

Darnell pulled her into a bear hug and dropped a peck on the top of her head. "S'all good, Doc. He'll be okay. Kash is a good guy."

Carl squeezed her from behind. "So...sooo good. He like...likes you."

"He does like you," Marty reassured, rubbing her arms. "He's been through a lot in just two weeks. I'd be inclined to cut him some slack, if you can. Especially because he knows this is about you. I respected that statement."

Scotty nodded, miserable. "Me, too."

"So give him a hot second, okay, Doc? All will be well. Trust the fucking vampire," Nina said, dropping a kiss on top of her head before heading out the door. "C'mon, Carl, let's go see what Arch's up to in the kitchen at the guesthouse."

As everyone followed suit, leaving her to sit with her emotions, Scotty sat down on the chair at her desk, burying her head in her hands.

What had she done?

And why did she still feel so damn weird?

"Hey, Burgermeister. Guess what, dude?"

Kash, lost deep in his dark thoughts about Scotty dying, welcomed the intrusion of Nina's voice. He looked down at the snow-covered ground beneath the deck at Marty's guesthouse. "What?"

She clapped him on the back. "We found your flashy man-car."

In all this, he'd forgotten about his car. A car that had once been one of his prized possessions—the one he'd been so proud of paying cash for—had been lost in much bigger things.

He'd all but forgotten about his restaurants, too. Also something he'd once fretted over day and night. It was why he'd only agreed to semi-retire—because he and Garrick had built Brother's from the ground up, and now here they were ten years later, looking to expand abroad.

But did that matter today, when what he'd heard had gut-punched him so hard, he didn't think he'd be able to stay standing?

It just went to show you, money bought things

that made you comfortable. Friends, family, and love brought you things that made you feel like you belonged. They brought fulfillment.

And he had to admit, being here with these people who'd dropped everything to help him—no charge, no strings—he felt fulfilled.

He felt like he belonged in this world, as though he'd been meant to get into that fight in the bar. But *none* of it felt right without Scotty in the picture he'd created in his mind.

"Dude? Didja hear me? We found your hot rod."

He turned around and leaned on the railing of the small deck in the backyard. "No way. Where was it? Was some demon joy-riding in it?"

Nina cackled. "Nope. It was in the impound, but we got it the fuck out not much worse for the wear. It's in the driveway, if you wanna see it."

It all seemed so unimportant at this point. "I'll take a look later," he said, knowing his voice sounded dull and defeated.

ScottyisdyingScottyisdyingScottyisdying.

That was all he could think about. He almost couldn't breathe from replaying the conversation she'd had with Nina over and over in his head. He suspected she had a disease of some kind, but he never imagined it meant she'd die.

How could she die when he hadn't been able to convince her to get to know him?

Yeah. How selfish of her. How dare she die when you haven't gotten what you want, you prick?

Jesus. No kidding it was selfish. He mostly understood why she didn't tell him—why she'd made such an effort to keep things strictly professional—but if he were allowed one selfish moment, Kash was glad he wasn't wrong about that kiss.

Because he'd felt like a total idiot after nearly demanding they'd had a moment.

Nina clapped him on the back again. "Hey, you okay? I thought you'd be fucking over the moon about us finding your ride. Thought it might cheer you the fuck up. It's a pretty sweet car."

Two weeks ago, he might have thought the same thing. "To be honest, I forgot all about it, but I appreciate it. There's been so much going on, it lost its rank in priority, I guess."

"Coming from a guy sprouting shit from every place on his body, I could see that."

They were silent a moment, and then he asked, "Did you know?"

She eyeballed him, stuffing her hands in her hoodie's kangaroo pocket. "About?"

"About Scotty...dying."

Jesus, he could hardly think the word, let alone say it out loud.

She shrugged, looking out into the backyard where Janet and Waffles had enjoyed many a run through the snow. "Yeah. I knew."

Rubbing a hand over his temples, Kash pinched them hard to thwart the headache he had building. "How can I feel so deeply about someone I hardly know?"

"I think sometimes when ya know, ya just know."

He laughed a bitter laugh, one filled with the irony of all this. "Is it the life mate thing?"

She leaned her elbows on the railing, knocking the snow off to sprinkle to the ground. "You know, before all this happened to me, I didn't believe in that shit. But I've been doing this for a while now. A good fucking long while, and I've changed my mind. I think that bullshit platitude that everything happens for a reason isn't such bullshit. Marrying Greg fit like a glove. We just work. Living this life with him—with them—changed my mind."

"Besides the obvious, how? How did it change your life?"

"Did Marty tell you how we all fucking met?"

He smiled at the memory she'd shared of her selling Bobbie-Sue cosmetics and recruiting Nina and Wanda as salesgirls. It sounded ludicrous—the bit about Nina and color wheels and her hatred of the color yellow. But look what it had turned into.

"She did."

"I never had much family, not even any friends really. Not real ones anyway. It was mostly me and my grandma Lou all my life. I was a loner with a dad who was always on the road and a bum-ass druggie

235

for a mother who left when I was a kid, just like you."

His immediate response was to apologize the way everyone did when he told his origin story, but he caught himself.

So he simply nodded in solidarity.

"I took that side gig selling Bobbie-Sue with Blondie in there to help make ends meet, not to be turned into a fucking vampire. But after it happened, the two people in the world I thought were too shallow and girly for a bad bitch loner like me turned out to be two of the best friends I've ever had. Along the way, we met people like Darnell, Carl, and Arch, and we all bonded. I've never had so many people have my back the way all of them in there do. We call ourselves framily."

He looked into the French doors at everyone gathered at the dining room table. It had become a sort of tradition after a long day in the lab to come back, sit at the lengthy table meant for large gatherings, and have a cup of coffee or tea with whatever tasty treat Arch had whipped up while they were gone.

Janet and Waffles sat under the table, while Espy perched on the back of the couch, watched over them. It all felt right.

They laughed about their triumphs, they moaned over disappointments, they shared their days, and when they did, he felt the blanket of solitude he'd never even recognized as loneliness being pulled away.

He'd never had that before. It had always been just him and Garrick, and then Janet. Now, he wasn't sure what he'd do without these people when it was over, when he had to go back to his old life, but for right now, they felt right.

Hearing Nina's words left his chest tight. "I was so wrong."

She leaned into him. "About?"

"About all of you. I'm probably not telling you anything new, but I thought you guys were a cult. I was wrong, and I want to apologize."

She laughed. "Not fucking necessary. You're not the first, probably won't be the last."

But Kash shook his head. "I still need to own my bias, and I had plenty of 'em."

"I did, too. You have no idea how fucking nutballs I thought these people were. We get it. It's the convincing that drives me nuts. I mean, like, what more do you fucking need to see than Marty all hairy and drooling the fuck all over you?"

He barked a laugh. "Fair question. Regardless, I don't think I can ever repay you for what you've done for me. There isn't a way to properly thank you guys for uprooting your lives the way you have."

"You can thank us by living a fucking happy life, despite your weird-ass afflictions. I think part of that life is supposed to be with Scotty. I don't know for how long. I don't know what shit will go down along the way, but I think you gotta give it a shot."

"Oddly, that was never a question for me. It's Scotty who told me to back off, and I respected that."

"She's scared, dude," Nina said quietly. "Aside from the fact that she has this kooky disease, she's also human. You're not anymore, so you'd outlive her whether she was sick or not. There's a lot to consider, and being logical, she's trying to make it as simple as possible, and force it all to make some fucking sense. Not to mention, that asshole of an ex fucked her over but good. She's skittish because of him."

The mere mention of that dick's name made him tense with anger. "What happened with Glen?"

"How about you ask her? For now, just give her a minute like she's giving you one."

His chest went tight. To hide the emotion he felt, Kash gave Nina a quick, hard hug. "Look at Nina-zilla with all the words tonight."

She squeezed him back then shoved him away. "Fuck off, weirdo."

He laughed out loud. "There she is."

"You okay now?"

"I think so."

"Fuck yeah. Atta boy. Dinner's gonna be ready soon. Arch said to tell you it's shepherd's pie night. Whatever the fuck that means."

He grinned. He'd mentioned that it was a favorite of his, and he missed making it.

"Tell him I'll be right in."

"You got it." She turned to go back inside the French doors, running into Scotty on the way.

"Mind if I join you?" she asked softly.

It's now or never, Kash.

Make it count.

CHAPTER

TWENTY-TWO

"You wanna take a walk?" he asked, holding out a hand to her.

Nina popped open the French doors again and called from inside, "Stay close, you two. Right the fuck where I can see you."

Scotty gave Nina the thumbs up and took Kash's hand, letting him lead her down the couple of steps facing the woods.

"You warm enough?" he asked, gripping her hand.

"I'm fine." She nodded and burrowed deep into her down jacket.

When they reached a patch of snow right in front of the dining room windows, he stopped, the moonlight catching the stubble on his face. His large frame loomed under the stars of the night sky, handsome and sturdy.

She pulled a small stuffed toy from her pocket and

smiled at him. "I forgot. Darnell found this on the floor of your car."

She held up what, if she remembered correctly, was a stuffed version of Lambchop like the one from the TV show. It had seen better days. Its fur was matted and one eye was a little crooked, but it felt worn with love.

He chuckled and took it from her fingers, pressing it to his chest. "Lambie! I forgot he was in the car. How could I forget Lambie?"

She smiled at the change in his face and the light-hearted tone of his voice. "Lambie?"

His smile was wistful and far away. "My one constant. It was the only thing I never forgot to take with me when we moved from foster home to foster home. I've had him since I was five, when they took us from my mother. I don't know where he came from or if she even got it for me, but I've never been without him."

Her heart went tight in her chest and her eyes stung with tears for a small boy with nowhere to call home. "That's really sweet."

He tucked Lambie into his jacket, his eyes searching hers. "Let me just get this out, okay? Then I'll shut up and you can say whatever you want and I won't interrupt."

"You have the talking stick."

Kash took both of her hands in his, her fingers cold, and cleared his throat. "I don't care that you're dying. I mean—wait. I care." He held up a hand. "But it doesn't make me any less inclined to want to get to know you.

"I felt something that night when we kissed, Scotty. Something clicked into place and the world was suddenly gone. Everything melted away except for you. I don't know what it means, I only know it means *something*. Something I've never felt. Something I'm almost positive I'll never feel again. I don't understand it, because we hardly know each other, but I want it just the same."

There was a long pause while she absorbed his words. Words that soothed her soul, eased the anxiety she'd built up all day while she'd waited to talk to him.

She'd thought about Nina's words for hours. She'd thought about what it would be like to go into this knowing he'd end up alone...and she still wanted him. Because he made her laugh. Because he was solid and he loved his brother and he'd never had anywhere to call home. Because he had a Lambie.

Because.

That was all she had for now. Maybe that would be enough.

"Ditto."

He studied her, cupping her face in his hands. "That's it? You don't want to talk it over? Set ground rules? Limits? Nothing?"

She gripped his wrists and grinned, feeling a little

giddy about letting go. "Nope. I say we live and let live —for as long as I'm alive, anyway."

He winced. "I'm not ready to laugh about it yet, but I do want to hear about it and what it all means. Are you ready to tell me?"

"I think I am."

"Okay, then. We're gonna try this? It's official?" His lips lingered maddeningly near hers, making her heart start that weird chugging.

"Uh-huh," she whispered breathlessly. "Whatever *this* is."

"I think this is called I'm your boyfriend."

She giggled. "That has a nice ring to it. Guess that means I'm your girlfriend," Scotty said, her lips barely brushing his. "Do boyfriends kiss their girlfriends?"

"Jesus Christ, Burgermeister, kiss the girl!" Nina crowed from the window where everyone had gathered, crowding their way into the small space.

"Kiss her! Kiss her!" Marty and Wanda cheered, with big smiles on their face.

"I think we should give them what they want."

Scotty didn't answer. Instead, she planted one on him while everyone cheered.

Then that melty thing happened, and she forgot about everyone and everything but Kash.

THEY STAYED UP ALL NIGHT, just talking, with Janet curled at the foot of her bed and Espy between them.

Scotty told him everything, from birth to Glen.

And he filled in the blanks after foster care right up until just two weeks ago when he'd been out for a drive, trying to wrap his head around semi-retirement.

"So that's why you were all the way out here?"

He pressed his fingers to hers, making a bridge over a soundly sleeping Espy. "Yep. I'm not used to not getting up at five every morning. I felt at loose ends, with no purpose, but I figured if I was ever going to have a personal life, I might want to reprioritize."

"Ah. All work, no play. I get it. I'm the same way. I've been working to try and find a cure for my disease, but no such luck so far. It's been a long, isolating road."

Kash brushed her hair from her face with gentle fingers. "I'm sorry. But I'm here now, for whatever that's worth. I'll be here as long as you let me."

She smiled, feeling so sleepy but reluctant to let him go.

He drew a finger over her cheek tenderly. "You need sleep, Scotty. You want to be wide awake to see what I shift into tomorrow, don't you? I mean, who knows what else I could turn into."

She rubbed her eyes and yawned. "You know, I still don't get the skinwalker thing. Like, how random."

"I don't either, but get some rest and we'll talk more about it tomorrow in the lab, okay?"

Tucking her hand under her chin, Scotty nodded and muttered, "Okay."

She felt Kash pull the covers up and over her and then Janet snuggle down next to her in the curve of her knees.

Scotty sighed with contentment when he pressed a kiss to the side of her lips, and tried to focus on how good his lips felt and ignore how weird *she* felt.

Because as Nina would say, GD it all, she still felt so fucking weird.

TWENTY-THREE

T he next day, they made their way to the lab together, holding hands and sleepily laughing at the things they'd shared last night.

Her heart had skipped a beat when Kash knocked on her door at seven this morning, showered and ready to have some breakfast before they began another long day in the lab.

"Right behind you guys!" Marty called with a wave.

"Babysitter walking!" Scotty called, feeling lighter than she had in days.

Kash pulled the lab door open for her, motioning she should go first. As she stepped inside, she was surprised to find Trina already there.

Scotty stopped dead in her tracks, looking around. "Um, what's happening?"

She flipped a hand upward at them, her wings buzzing colorfully behind her. "Hey, Boss."

"You're early."

Trina put her hands on her hips. "You say that like it's a bad thing."

Scotty instantly checked herself. Trina showing up early showed enthusiasm, and she wasn't going to discourage it by reminding her of her poor performance thus far.

Giving Trina a light tap on the back, she smiled and shook her head. "Nope. It's an awesome thing. Thanks for being here."

Kash grinned at her and hopped up on the examining table. "Mornin', Trina."

Trina gave them an odd look. "What's going on here? Why is the vibe so light today? Usually it's all angsty and brooding, pouting and sneaking glances at each other when you think no one's looking. Wait!" she said, holding up a hand with a smug smile. "Did you guys bang this out?"

"Trina!" Scotty gasped.

Rolling her eyes, she went back to what she was doing on the desk. "Oh, fine. Don't tell me. Whatever. I have to go get more syringes anyway. I know you have the super sadsies when we're low, don't you, good-lookin'?"

Kash actually laughed at her teasing about his contempt for needles and blood. "Cryin' on the inside," he joked back.

Trina made her exit seconds before Kash checked to see if the coast was clear, latching onto her arm and pulling her in close.

"Did we say good morning properly?" he asked against her lips.

She sighed happily, stretching her arms around his neck and leaning into him. "I can't remember. Why don't you remind me?"

He swooped down, slanting his lips over hers, pulling her firmly against his torso.

Phew, his lips were made of magic. As she sank into him, she remembered they had work to do, and as much as she'd like to continue this make-out session, they were never going to accomplish anything if they kept this up.

Pulling away, she pressed her fingers to his lips. "We have to stop. We have work to do."

"But whyyyy?" he whined on a chuckle, his dark hair falling over his forehead when he let his head fall back on his shoulders dramatically.

She snorted. "Listen, if you behave and do all yours tests today, I'll teach you how to style your lovely locks."

Grabbing a strand of pink hair that had hung around since yesterday's sudden shift, he shook it at her, giving her one last kiss. "Promises, promises. Okay, so what's on tap today?"

She looked at her watch as he let her feet touch the

floor, rolling her head back and forth. Man, she had a headache.

"Blood tests. I know how much you hate 'em, but I have a couple more a colleague suggested that might help us sort some stuff out. Also, maybe you can tell me again what you were visualizing yesterday when you shifted into a merman."

"A colleague?"

"Don't worry. He can be trusted. Promise. He's an old college professor. I'd trust him with my life."

He appeared to relax a little. "So what do you think's on today's menu. Ya think we could work out this thing coming out of my back? Because it's like sleeping on a rock."

She ran her fingers over the partial wing, still solidly stuck in place with no sign of changing.

"Focus," she reminded. "Now one more time, what were you thinking about yesterday when you sprouted a fin? Maybe think dragon things? Like fire breathing and living in caves."

Kash laughed, his eyes crinkling up. "But what if it's an angel wing?"

"Then think pure things," she said with a coy smile.

He winked. "Don't know if that's possible around you."

A rush of happiness swept up her spine and she fought a breathy giggle. Focusing wasn't going to be easy. "What the heck is taking Trina so long?"

Scotty began to cross the floor to go find Trina when her legs quite suddenly felt like noodles. Her heart began to race and a cold sweat trickled between her breasts.

Stumbling, she fell against the lab door, flushed with heat, crashing against it with her shoulder so hard, it cracked open slightly, only to be stopped by something heavy pressed up against the other side.

She saw a flash of blonde hair and some bangle bracelets.

Marty? She wanted to call out her name, but she couldn't make her tongue work.

"Scotty!" Kash called out, hopping off the lab table and racing to her side.

His strong hands gathered her up and she was useless to do anything to aid him. Her body went boneless like limp spaghetti.

What the hell was going on?

Kash ran a finger down her cheek as he held her on the floor. "Scotty, what's happening?"

But she couldn't answer. Her lips wouldn't move, she was paralyzed—and that meant she couldn't warn him that Marty was slumped on the floor, blocking their exit out of the lab.

He was so busy looking down at her, she couldn't even warn him that *another* Marty was pushing her way into the door with a long, shiny needle.

An imposter Marty? Was this the skinwalker thing? Because it was freaky as hell! And Kash was so focused on her, he hadn't even glanced toward the lab door.

Her mind raced as she tried to blink her eyes —*something.*

But nothing stopped the imposter from raising the needle high in the air and jabbing Kash in the neck.

Instantly, his body went as limp as hers while she helplessly watched fake Marty carry him out the door. Then someone she couldn't see grabbed her under her armpits and dragged her out of the lab, too.

And today had started off so well...

KASH WOKE WITH A START, his eyes popping open as though someone had jolted him with a cattle prod.

Trying to sit up, he found himself strapped to a table. Yanking at the cuffs around his wrists, he tried with no luck to pull them loose.

What the hell was going on?

Twisting his head from side to side, Kash tried to see what was around him. He was definitely in a hospital of some kind. A windowless room with nothing more than a prep table and some shiny metal, floating countertop.

Maybe something had happened when they were preparing to do more tests and he'd landed in the ER?

But no... Like whiplash, he remembered Scotty falling on the floor, gathering her up, panicking that she was hurt. She'd lay limp in his arms, her eye wide open, her limbs unmoving.

But she'd had a pulse. He remembered that.

Straining as far forward as he could, he caught sight of another bed across the room, on the opposite wall. A long strand of dark hair draped over the side of the bed.

Scotty? Looking down the length of her body, he noted the boots she'd worn today were still on her feet.

Fear surged in his gut. What the fuck was happening? "Scotty? Scotty! Wake up!"

But there was no response from the other side of the room. Shit!

Okay, think, Kash. Think. Visualize freeing yourself. Tugging against the handcuffs, he pulled as hard as he could.

For whatever random reason, he thought about Superman, breaking free of his chains. He thought about the comparison one of the ladies had made to the Hulk, and ripping them off. He visualized every superhero he could think of, and all for naught.

"Fuck!" he seethed.

"Oh, you'll never get out of them," a cultured voice drawled, making him twist his head back in the direction of the door.

Seriously?

"Bet you didn't expect to see me today, did you?"

Well, son-of-a-bitch.

G‌LEN?

Scotty heard his voice. She also heard Kash's, but she had no idea where she was or what was going on.

And why couldn't she move?

Rushes of heat assaulted her body. Hot waves of blood coursing through her veins kept her immobile while surge after surge of some invisible entity slithered in her belly. But nothing moved, not even an eyeball. Jesus, what was happening to her?

Think, Scotty. Think. Where are you and why is Glen here?

"You'll never get loose from those, Kash. They're silver. To keep the were in you contained. So sit back and enjoy the ride. You're gonna make me a lot of money, buddy."

Wait, *what*? Glen had Kash handcuffed in silver?

What in all of bondage was going on here?

"Why is Scotty here? What the fuck's going on?" Kash seethed.

She heard Glen scoff. "Well, she wasn't part of the plan, but every once in a while there's an old hitch in the giddy-up, you know? So we go with plan B. She'd out cold, so it doesn't matter anyway."

"What have you done to her?" Kash demanded, making Scotty's heart chug harder.

"I didn't do anything to her. My guy found her like that when he came to collect you. So rather than have collateral damage, we'll just eliminate that problem altogether."

"Your guy?"

She heard the strain in Kash's voice, sensed he was growing angrier by the second, but she couldn't do anything to stop it.

The question was, did she want to stop it? Why was Kash restrained? What money was Glen talking about?

"Yeah, *my guy*. I sent someone to retrieve you. I didn't get to this point in my career by doing the dirty work. The first one failed, and he'll pay dearly for it, but the second was successful and that's all that matters."

Suddenly, she understood, and so did Kash because as her mind was screaming, Kash yelped, "Nina? You sent a skinwalker in to pose as Nina?"

Leave it to Glen to find a skinwalker. Didn't Wanda say they were incredibly rare?

"Well, yeah. I mean, it worked, didn't it? For a minute anyway. But then he did something stupid." He paused a moment and clucked his tongue. "Bah, neither here nor there. I knew the second Banner told me the OOPS women had requested Scotia that something important was up, and I was right."

Kash was gritting his teeth. Scotty could almost hear them grind. "Look, I don't know what you plan to do with me, but let her go."

"I plan to make a lot of money off you. That's what I plan to do," Glen responded.

"Money?" Kash hissed. "What the hell are you talking about? How can I make you money?"

She heard Glen suck his teeth, and she'd bet he was rocking back on his heels the way he always did when he had some brilliant financial coup in mind. "You're very special, Kash. Very special indeed, and worth a lot of money to...uh, people. Unsavory though they might be."

Kash's voice was tight when he asked, "Do I get to know what makes me so special?"

Yeah? Do we get to know? Scotty wanted to scream, but no sound was coming from her throat.

"All in due time, pal. Until then, relax. Enjoy the ride. If I know Scotty, she dogged you until you wanted to tear your damn hair out so she could figure out what to do with you. How to fix her little freak."

Oh, fuck you, Glen!

TWENTY-FOUR

"I think the gentlemanly thing to do is to tell me what you're going to do with me, don't you? What do you know about my new status that I don't?" Kash prompted.

His tone had gone from tense to so tight, you could bounce a quarter off it.

"I'm surprised Scotty didn't figure it out. Though, to be fair to her scientific skills, you're extremely rare and you haven't shown all your true colors yet. There isn't much documentation on those of your type. But you're gonna help a dying breed, Kash. You'll be a real hero. Just you wait and see."

Okay, what hadn't she figured out? If he was extremely rare, was he a skinwalker? No! That couldn't be. She'd tested him. He showed no signs of anything other than the usual laundry list of paranormals.

"Explain my type..."

Please. For the people in the back.

"You're a chimera, buddy. A rare breed of hybrid chimera, capable of shifting into almost anything. It's not the typical breed, of course. It's my understanding it's quite a complex explanation. You'll have abilities far beyond the normal chimera."

A chimera.

This is what she got for not keeping her lips to herself. She'd been so distracted, wowed by how handsome he was, that she'd missed the idea of chimera completely. But Glen said he was a hybrid. What did this all mean?

"What the hell is that?" Kash ground out.

It should be her explaining it to him, not stupid-face Glen.

"It's why you have all these things sticking out of you. A fin, a tail, the pink hair...it means you can shift into different animals and species of the paranormal. You can do it all, Kash. Though your success has been a bit thwarted, that'll change. Thanks to Trina and a handsome price, which I'll take back when I get rid of her, I was able to procure a sample of your blood and have someone with experience in the area take a look. Easy-peasy."

Trina? Trina had sold Kash's blood samples to Glen? Maybe that explained why Kash had gone after her that day when he broke the tank?

Because he smelled Trina's deception? He'd said he couldn't pinpoint the smell, but it wouldn't be unheard of that a paranormal was sensitive to something like that...

Oh my God, this smug bastard! If she ever got out of here, she was going to knock the shit out of him and dig out his liver so Nina could eat it with crackers, and Trina wouldn't be far behind.

Then her thoughts went to Kash. He must be reeling from this new information. Finally learning what he was...that was huge.

"Trina gave me up?"

Glen barked a laugh. "You sound surprised. Trina'd sell her soul for a buck. She was an easy mark." He sighed, sounding rather bored. "Listen, I don't know how the hell it happened, I don't know how it's even possible, but here you are and just in the nick of time. You're going to help make a new breed of chimeras for as long as the others need you to."

"And then?" Kash asked.

"Then they'll do away with you—just like what should have happened from the start. I'll never understand this new brand of tolerance those OOPS women preach. It's unacceptable. Unless it pays. Then I'm happy as a clam to provide."

Jesus, she knew Glen could be a coldhearted prick. He *did* break up with her over the phone. But killing people? She wondered how much Banner McNealy would like his connections now.

She had to do something—anything—but by hell, she couldn't move even a half inch.

Another pulse of heat raced to her toes and zinged back up toward her head, which had taken to throbbing to a beat all its own.

"So am I going to be some kind of breeder for these chimera people?"

"People? There's only two or three of them left and they've had zero success procreating. That's why you're so important. So, if that's how you want to look at it, sure. You'll be a real stallion."

"How do you know I'll be able to procreate?" Kash spat, his tone brimming with tension.

"I think they mentioned something about your blood and some special cell or strand of DNA." He shrugged. "I don't really know what it was. I just know they liked what they saw in your blood, and I have half the money, so I don't really care."

If anyone in the universe was listening, she hoped they were hearing her silent pleas to get her the hell off this table. No one knew where they were. *She* didn't even know where they were.

Mingled with all the rushes of hot and cold in her body came fear. Leave it to fucking Glen to try to steal the happiness she'd found meeting Kash. Just when things were looking up a tiny bit.

Oooo, she wanted to strangle the asshole.

"You know you'll get caught, don't you?" Kash sounded so sure of his threat. "Those women will never let this rest. If the tales about them are true, you're fucked when they find out you hurt Scotty."

"Blah, blah, blah. They're never going to find out who took her. Worry not. Anyway, this has been nice, but I'm going to leave you in the hands of the people who *really* want to meet you."

"Let Scotty go!" Kash bellowed, but his words fell on deaf ears. Glen was already on his way out the door.

Seeing his back from her prone position on the bed incited her. Ravaged her guts until they felt like a plate of spaghetti.

That was when it happened.

Whatever had a hold on her, whatever had clutched her in its grip for the last week, suddenly let loose—and she exploded off the bed, the sheet falling away to the floor.

On her feet, she heard herself growl.

Growl? What in all of hell was going on?

Yet, it happened again when she went to call Glen's name. "Glen! Get back here, you stupid bastard!"

Scotty's eyes flew open wide as she doubled over and fell to the floor on her hands and knees. Looking down, her chest heaving, she saw her hands turn into paws. Big, hairy paws.

All at once, her head felt like it weighed more than a ton of bricks and the noise swirling around in there sounded like a freight train.

She lifted her enormous head—God, how did Marty do this?—and reared back. Her skull lolled wildly until she righted it, and then she set her gaze on Glen, paused in the doorway and staring at her in such obvious astonished horror, she'd have laughed if she were capable.

Vaulting forward, relishing the exhilarating strength thrumming through her veins, she had the element of surprise on her side when she ran at Glen. Charging him with a surprising amount of energy, Scotty went straight for his throat.

But she fumbled, tripping over her own big paws, giving Glen the moment he needed to get his bearings.

"Scotty?" he shouted, his shock evident right before he throat punched her to the ground, swatting her like a gnat.

That only served to further infuriate her. Yeah, Glen was the more experienced paranormal, he'd likely prevail, but not before she took a few good shots at him.

The power surging through her limbs left her feeling invincible, canceled out the pain of his swipe at her, and while she fumbled to steady herself in her new body, her mind whirled with questions.

Like, what the hell was happening to her? How had she done this? What would it all mean?

Yet, she didn't have time to think about the answers before Glen was shoving a helpless, confined

Kash out of the way, his bed crashing against the side wall.

And then Glen came for her, his fangs flashing in anger—fangs *she'd* helped save.

The shithead.

The menace in his stance, the anger in his howl when he screeched a high sound she'd never heard before, sent cold chills along her spine.

Then he had her by the neck, shaking her body as though she hadn't just shifted into a beast but a rag doll.

Her drool spattered everywhere, her eyes rattled in her head, but she fought back with a vengeance, taking a swipe at Glen's face, making him laugh at her awkward jab.

"You dumb bitch!" he hollered, his face a mask of hatred as he threw her against the far wall. "You'll never get out of here alive, you fool!"

She took the brunt of the wall against her back, hearing her bones crack and her spine bend before she bounced off the surface and rolled across the floor, but his words only made her angrier.

Apparently, his words made Kash angry, too.

Because he called out, "Duck, Scotty!" followed by —oh, holy shit—a fireball the size of a basketball.

It sizzled as it screamed past her head and managed to singe Glen's perfect blond hair.

Well. Guess they didn't have to wonder what that wing on Kash's back was anymore, did they?

Kash could see nothing but red and Scotty, shifted into an enormous werewolf to rival Marty, now in danger as Glen hurled her around the room like some kind of plastic bag.

And it made him want to kill the motherfucker.

Something deep inside him welled up and rose to the surface, an angry wave of rage, insidious, twisting inside him until he bellowed—and out shot of ball of fire.

Amazed and horrified at the same time, he realized what he'd done. Then he set to work to get his hands on Glen. Yanking his wrist upward as far as he could, he blew on the lengths of cuffs retraining him, easily melting them and breaking the bond.

He dropped off the table and leapt across the room, headfirst for Glen, bashing into him and nearly doubling him in half. Glen slammed into the wall with a howl, his eyes shiny with hate.

And he wasn't going down without a fight. Wrapping his arms around Kash's back, he steamrolled him out the door and into a room where people scattered, their feet stomping on the tile floor.

Kash skidded to the far wall on his back, his eyes flying past feet and desk legs, chairs. His head snapped against the wall, cracking it hard, leaving his blood flying everywhere.

Then Glen stood over him, pointing a gun in his

face, while Kash gasped for air. "Don't move or I swear to Christ, I'll blow your stupid pink head off!"

Seething, Kash fought for breath, his chest ready to explode as he stared at the butt of the gun.

Did gun beat dragon? Did he dare find out?

He couldn't see Scotty anymore, but he heard her gasping for breath when the room finally cleared and everything else went silent. As he looked at the wreckage of their fight, the gun in his face, all he could think about was Scotty's safety.

And for that, he'd bargain.

"Do whatever you want to me, but leave Scotty alone. Disappear, do whatever you have to, but don't hurt her. *Please*."

Glen grabbed his arm, yanking him upward and shoving him back against the wall. Kash's lip was split and swollen, his dilapidated wing crushed behind him.

"Shut the fuck up about her and move it, Lover Boy! We have somewhere to be and I have money to collect."

It was then he heard a hiss. A strange sound...like air releasing from a balloon. The room went still as a black shadow slipped across the floor, rattling and wending its way toward them.

Kash's mouth fell open.

He must have looked surprised enough that he caught Glen off guard. The vampire whipped around.

Just as the black shadow slithered up inside his fancy pants with their pristine creases.

There was a lump at his crotch, right where his business nested, pushing his pants outward before sinking into his pelvic area.

Glen screamed so loud, the windows in the room shook. *"Get it the fuck off me!"* His hands instinctively went to the apex at his thighs as he dropped the gun and began to twist and shake, trying to release whatever was in his pants.

Kash dove for the gun, sliding across the floor to grab it just as footsteps pounded into the room.

"Kash! Aw, man!" Darnell bounded into the room, his round face full of concern as he grabbed Glen by the collar and hauled him up. "What's going on?" he yelled over Glen's screeching.

"Get! It! Off!" Glen screeched again, tugging at his pants while still in Darnell's iron grip.

Kash held the gun limp at his side, still unable to process what he'd seen.

"Kash! Where's the doc?" Darnell shouted.

His mouth still open, he pointed at Glen's pants. "I think she's in there!"

"For Christ's sake, what's all the screaming about?" Nina called from the doorway as Trina buzzed behind her.

Marty and Wanda followed, rushing into the room on their fashionable heels.

It was just then that what he'd thought was Scotty dropped out of the leg of Glen's pants and skittered away.

Marty screamed and hopped into Nina's arms. "*Snaaake!*" she screeched.

Nina rolled her eyes. "Get the fuck off me, Blondie. That's Scotty, dumbass! Jesus and fuck, Marty. You're a damn werewolf. Act like it!"

Now Wanda's eyes went wide as she followed the shadow back into the other room. "*What?* That's Scotty?"

"I think so," Kash said, his response slathered in shock.

Nina dumped Marty on the floor and plucked Glen from Darnell's grip, holding his limp body up in the air so she could examine him.

"Shut the fuck up and stop whining, you asshole!" she demanded. "I've got some people you're gonna wanna meet."

Now that Kash had caught his breath, he headed straight for Scotty to see if she was all right. "Scotty!"

"In here!" she yelled.

He stopped dead when he realized she was nude, turning his back in respect.

"Wow. Shifting is hard on your clothes, huh?"

He didn't know why, but he burst out laughing. "Is that all you have to say for yourself?"

"Well, there's also the exfoliation factor. Ten out of ten."

"Can I turn around?"

"All clear."

Scotty had her clothes back on, a bit shredded but at least enough to cover her. There was a weird casing of some kind on the floor, as well as big tufts of hair blowing around.

He held his hands up to his head and flicked them open, mimicking an explosion. "Mind blown. What the hell just happened?"

She grinned at him, that coy grin that said she was pleased. "I have no idea. I've been feeling weird since you scratched me last week. I think I was in some weird kind of stasis, maybe? I was so angry that Glen had betrayed me not once, but twice, that I just kind've...exploded. All of a sudden, it just happened. There was teeth and hair and snarling drool. Then there was shedding and slithering and *shablam*!"

He strode across the room and reached for her, pulling her close and tucking her against his frame. "That snake? What is even happening?"

She leaned back in his arms and smiled. "You did hear Glen say you're a chimera, right?"

He nodded. "I did. I can shift into animals and people and... something?"

Scotty draped her arms around his neck. "Yep. But I think when you scratched me, somehow, you turned me, too."

Kash's eyes went wide. "So you're telling me you were kind of on the back burner, simmering? Like a caterpillar turning into a butterfly simmering? I thought you couldn't be turned?"

She squeezed the muscles in his arms and smiled. "I haven't had time to think about what could have caused this, but I'm pretty sure it's our unique mix of blood. Whatever it is, it worked. I don't know what it means for my disease or what this means for you and this rare breed of chimera Glen was talking about, but...here we are."

He hugged her hard against his chest as she buried her face in his neck. "That was incredible," he whispered.

"*You* were incredible," she praised, her heart thumping. "I think dragon it is, huh?"

Trina flew in then with Wanda and Marty close behind her, their faces stern. Tears streamed down her face as her wings fluttered. "Scotty, I'm sorry! I...I'm so sorry," she cried. "I didn't know he would hurt you!"

"Trina..." Scotty said, but it was clear she didn't know what to say.

"Trina Sutter?" a loud voice boomed.

Trina blanched. "You called my father?" she asked Marty and Wanda, her surprise obvious. "He's gonna kill me!"

"You bet your fluttery ass we did," Nina, stomping into the room, Glen still in her grip. "Now take her out of here before I pluck her little wings right the fuck off!"

"I can't believe Trina sold us out," Kash muttered, tucking her to his side.

Scotty blew out a breath. "I wish I could say I don't believe it either, but I do." Then she shook her head. "Let's not think about her now. What I want to know is, how did you guys know where we were?"

Darnell gave her a quick squeeze. "Believe it or not, Trina. She got scared when those fools Glen was workin' with took you, too. They were only s'posed to take Kash. So she followed 'em and texted us."

Nina gave a limp Glen a hard shake. "You fucking idiot. You didn't cover your tracks. Why are you such an asshole? You give vampires everywhere a bad name, fucknuts."

"I'll take him," Banner McNealy said, striding into the room, heading directly toward Scotty.

"Dad?" she said breathlessly.

He smiled and gave her a quick hug before pointing to Glen, his lean face hard and angry. "*You will pay.*"

He snatched Glen from Nina's hands and dragged him toward the door, where two big men waited to take him. "Lunch soon, honey, yes?"

"Yes!" she yelled back, her face beaming.

"Bring the young man. We'll get to know each other," he declared over his shoulder before he and the other men were gone, taking Glen with them.

Silence fell over the room as all that had passed set

in—and then Nina clapped her hands and said, "Okay, let's get you two the fuck out of here. I have shit to do."

"Wait!" Scotty stopped as everyone began to file out.

"Now what?" Nina groaned.

She launched herself at Nina. "Group hug!"

Everyone gathered around Scotty and Kash, patting each other on the backs and laughing at Nina, who tried to get free.

"Get the fuck off me, people!" she yelped, pulling her long limbs from the tangle of bodies, but she was laughing, too.

Kash broke free first, taking Scotty by the hand and leading her out the door. "So where do you think we should go on our first date? What does a snake like to eat?"

She laughed out loud, her head falling back on her shoulders, making Kash smile. "I dunno, but I know this cute guy who has a burger restaurant with fries that I hear are to die for. Whaddya think?"

"A cute guy, you say?" he whispered, pulling her close once more, brushing her hair from her face. "Should I be jealous?"

"Well, he does have burgers," she teased against his lips.

"But can he breathe fire? That really is the question du jour. I don't want to brag, but I—me, right here—can breathe *fire*."

She smiled up at him. "You know, I meant to ask, does that leave an aftertaste?"

Kash, his chest tight, his world changed forever, leaned down, leaving his lips close to hers. "How about you tell me?" he murmured before he kissed her.

Thoroughly.

Completely.

EPILOGUE

*E*leven months later...

One chimera who made out-of-this-world burgers and had an awesome dog name Janet; a research scientist who'd fallen wildly in love with a chimera and his dog and could shift into a fierce serpent and a savage werewolf (so far); a troll who loved to cater a good party; a blonde werewolf who was terrified of snakes; a vampire who thought it was hysterical her BFF was afraid of snakes; a half-werewolf, half-vampire who was constantly mediating arguments between the werewolf and the vampire; and a sweet zombie who loved to help his new chimera friend cook, all gathered on a cool fall day for a surprise party at a little place called Brother's Burgers...

. . .

Nina told Kash and Scotty to open their eyes while leading them into a place that smelled very familiar to her because she'd spent many, many nights here with Kash.

Her stomach growled in hunger as Marty, Darnell, Carl and Wanda hollered, "Surprise!"

Scotty smiled wide. "What have you guys done?" she breathed, her heart full as she saw everyone standing under a sign that read "Yay, You're Not Gonna Die—Welcome to the Family," including her parents.

Colorful balloons hung from the lanterns over each table at Kash's restaurant and streamers were strung around the ceiling.

"Well, well, Doc. Look who's gonna live?" Nina crowed, giving her a hard hug.

Scotty rolled her eyes and hugged Nina back, trying to keep her tears at bay. It was true. She wasn't going to die, and there were days she was so grateful, she almost couldn't breathe from it.

She gave Nina a peck on the cheek and squeezed her hand. "Thanks, Marshmallow."

"Nina," Kash said, pressing a kiss to her cheek as well. "Is this what you guys have been up to all week? I wondered why I couldn't get in touch with anyone."

Nina and everyone else at OOPS had decided Kash needed some framily, as Nina called it, so they'd taken him under their wing and given him a genuine framily welcome.

They called him once a week, gave him advice, they had him and Scotty over for dinner, they invited them to all their family functions, leaving Kash over-whelmed with more love than any one person could handle.

But he loved it. He'd told her so one night when they were sitting by a warm fire after practicing their shifts, sharing a bottle of wine and a big steak.

He'd told her how glad he was he'd walked into that bar that night. That it had been worth all the fear and uncertainty to come out the other end with these people by his side.

"Jesus and a fucking production," Nina complained, shoving her hands into her jean pockets. "These nuts just couldn't settle the fuck down. They've been planning this shit with your brother since we found out Scotty's cleared for takeoff."

That day had been unforgettable. They'd all gath-ered around Marty's lab at Bobbie-Sue as they'd waited for the test results to find out if Scotty's disease was in fact in remission, and if all the kooky things going on in her body because of her new paranormal status were responsible.

When they'd all gotten the news, there had been a second of silence before they erupted in cheers, both Marty and Wanda in gulping tears, vowing there'd be a celebration to mark the happy occasion.

Since that horrible day when Glen tried to kill them, they'd grown closer than ever. She often reflected on how right Kash had been to insist they'd had a moment, that their kiss meant something, because ever since, she'd never once questioned how right it felt to be with him.

It was instantly right. They worked.

There were a lot of adjustments to be made, for sure. He was a complete control freak when it came to washing his whites with colors, and she threw it all in at once and hoped for the best.

She loved to sit out on his back patio and listen to Michael Bolton blasting in her earbuds, and he preferred the quiet solace of nature.

He was an early bird, and she was a night owl, often found hunkered down over one test result or another as she continued to try to find a cure for the disease that had once plagued her. But Kash made a point of bringing her dinner when she worked late, and she happily sipped wine as they made plans for what he'd do now that he wasn't as involved with the restaurant, but she still had a full-time career.

All of that late-night musing had led Kash to look into fostering paranormal children—to give them what he'd never had, however temporary—and she'd agreed he'd be an amazing foster parent.

There was also the question of a playmate for Janet and Espy, and they'd been scouring the local shelter for the right fit.

"Hey, where's Garrick?" Kash asked the girls, who pointed across the room to Scotty's mother and father, laughing at something his brother was saying.

As dark as Kash, he was handsome and funny, and Scotty liked him a lot. Garrick was still adjusting to the very idea of the paranormal, but he was coming around just fine.

Especially seeing as Kash's wings did turn out to be dragon wings and, according to his brother, that was pretty cool.

When they'd finally gotten the details about what they were—this rare breed of chimera that meant they could shift into almost anything—they'd both set out to discover their abilities together.

And wow, what a trip. They'd each worked hard together to learn how to perfect their shifts. So far, Scotty had only been able to manage to perfect were-wolf and serpent. Her vampire was iffy at best. Still, she'd gained about twenty pounds from eating more steak than a pasture of cows could provide, but Kash claimed it looked goon on her, and she felt more alive, and sexier than she'd ever felt before.

As for Kash? He was a real over-achiever. He could shift into a table lamp given enough time to visualize properly.

"Hey, did you hear the news about Trina?" Marty asked, her blonde hair shiny under the lights of the restaurant.

Scotty nodded, grateful her ex-assistant had received a fairly light sentence from her council. Trina had sent a message via her father, profusely apologizing again, and while Scotty was still angry, both she and Kash decided their lives were going to be pretty long, so—why hold a grudge? Besides, Marty claimed it gave you wrinkles.

Glen, though? Glen was in deep trouble, not only for the trafficking of Kash, but crimes they'd uncovered after his arrest by the vampire council. Things like embezzlement and money laundering, to name but a few. He wouldn't see the outside of a vampire prison for an eternity.

"Sweet girl!" her father called out, making his way across the red concrete floor to envelope her in a warm hug.

They, too, had managed to work through her childhood hurts, and with therapy, her mother and father were happier than ever.

She hugged him hard. "Hey, Dad! Did you know about this?"

He grinned, looking more carefree than she'd ever seen him. "Indeed, I did, darling. We're so happy for you."

"Sir." Kash addressed Banner with a smile and a shake of his hand. "Good to see you."

Banner reached out and pulled Kash into a hug. "Good to see you, too, son."

Kash and Banner had taken an instant liking to each other. They watched football games together whenever they could and were often found talking about Kash's venture into the foreign market for his restaurants. Banner gave him financial advice that Kash claimed had been priceless.

All in all, they were making their way through this crazy new world they shared, learning how to shift more efficiently, understanding what they were now capable of. Scotty was learning what it was like not to live with a disease that had ravaged her body—learning what it felt like to be strong—and it felt good.

Kash nudged her while she listened to the sounds of the people she loved laughing and talking, eating the food Arch had taken such care in preparing. "Hey."

She turned to him with a smile, her heart beating strong in her chest. "Uh-huh?"

"Have I told you how lucky I feel to have joined the cult?"

She laughed and ran her knuckles down his cheek. "Careful there, buddy, or I might start wondering if you drank the juice."

He barked a laugh. "Guilty, but I draw the line at handing out pamphlets at the airport. Got that?"

"So no tambourines and grapevine wreaths in your hair? Damn. Just when I was getting good at flower braiding."

Wrapping his arm around her, he pulled her to his side, a familiar place these days. A place where she always found comfort. "We've come a long way, haven't we?"

She pressed a kiss to his lips as an answer.

They sure had.
And now here they were, celebrating.
Life.
The love she and Kash had found.
Friends.
And framily.

THE END

ABOUT THE AUTHOR

Dakota Cassidy is a USA Today bestselling author with over almost one-hundred books. She writes laugh-out-loud cozy mysteries, romantic comedy, grab-some-ice erotic romance, hot and sexy alpha males, paranormal shifters, contemporary kick-ass women, and more.

Dakota lives in Texas with her real-life hero and her dogs, and she loves hearing from readers!

Join my newsletter: **The Tiara Diaries**

https://www.dakotacassidy.com/contact.html

Facebook

https://www.facebook.com/
DakotaCassidyFanPage

ALSO BY DAKOTA CASSIDY

Visit Dakota's website at http://www.
dakotacassidy.com for more information.

*A Lemon Layne Mystery, a Contemporary Cozy
Mystery Series*

1. Prawn of the Dead
2. Play That Funky Music White Koi

*Witchless In Seattle Mysteries, a Paranormal
Cozy Mystery series*

1. Witch Slapped
2. Quit Your Witchin'
3. Dewitched
4. The Old Witcheroo
5. How the Witch Stole Christmas
6. Ain't Love a Witch
7. Good Witch Hunting
8. Witch Way Did He Go?

9. Witches Get Stitches

10. Witch it Real Good

11. Witch Perfect

12. Gettin' Witched

13. Where There's a With, There's a Way

14. A Total Witch Show

Marshmallow Hollow Cozy Christmas Mysteries

1. Jingle All the Slay

2. Have Yourself a Merry Little Witness

3. One Corpse Open Slay

4. Carnage in a Pear Tree

Bewitching Midlife Crisis Mysteries (Paranormal Women's Fiction)

1. Stage Fright

Nun of Your Business Mysteries, a Paranormal Cozy Mystery series

1. Then There Were Nun

2. Hit and Nun

3. House of the Rising Nun

4. The Smoking Nun

5. What a Nunderful World

Wolf Mates, a Paranormal Romantic Comedy series

1. An American Werewolf In Hoboken

2. What's New, Pussycat?

3. Gotta Have Faith

4. Moves Like Jagger

5. Bad Case of Loving You

A Paris, Texas Romance, a Paranormal Romantic Comedy series

1. Witched At Birth
2. What Not to Were
3. Witch Is the New Black
4. White Witchmas

Non-Series

Whose Bride Is She Anyway?

Polanski Brothers: Home of Eternal Rest

Sexy Lips 66

Accidentally Paranormal Novel, a Paranormal Romantic Comedy series (published with Berkley Sensation)

1. The Accidental Werewolf
2. Accidentally Dead
3. The Accidental Human
4. Accidentally Demonic
5. Accidentally Catty
6. Accidentally Dead, Again
7. The Accidental Genie
8. The Accidental Werewolf 2: Something About Harry
9. The Accidental Dragon

The Accidentals, a Paranormal Romantic Comedy Series (self-published)

1. Accidentally Aphrodite
2. Accidentally Ever After
3. Bearly Accidental
4. How Nina Got Her Fang Back

5. The Accidental Familiar

6. Then Came Wanda with a Baby Carriage

7. The Accidental Mermaid

8. Marty's Horrible, Terrible Very Bad Day

9. The Accidental Unicorn

10. The Accidental Troll

11. Accidentally Divine

12. The Accidental Gargoyle

Plum Orchard, a Contemporary Romantic Comedy series

1. Talk This Way

2. Talk Dirty to Me

3. Something to Talk About

4. Talking After Midnight

The Ex-Trophy Wives, a Contemporary Romantic Comedy series

1. You Dropped a Blonde On Me

2. Burning Down the Spouse

3. Waltz This Way

Fangs of Anarchy, a Paranormal Urban Fantasy series

1. Forbidden Alpha

2. Outlaw Alpha

Made in the USA
Coppell, TX
10 September 2023

21444232R00164